Was It a Dream

A Collection of Real-Life Short Stories
by
Shirley Johnson Griffin

Daddy's diamond in the rough that never got polished!

PublishAmerica
Baltimore

© 2008 by Shirley Johnson Griffin.
All rights reserved. No part of this book may be reproduced, stored in a retrieval system or transmitted in any form or by any means without the prior written permission of the publishers, except by a reviewer who may quote brief passages in a review to be printed in a newspaper, magazine or journal.

First printing

PublishAmerica has allowed this work to remain exactly as the author intended, verbatim, without editorial input.

ISBN: 1-60610-825-5
PUBLISHED BY PUBLISHAMERICA, LLLP
www.publishamerica.com
Baltimore

Printed in the United States of America

Dedication

To: My Present and Future Family Members

I must thank God for this exceptional journey for which He has allowed me to travel/ I thank my father and mother, Thomas Newton and Louise Amanda Tolbert Johnson for allowing me the freedom to find my way through this life.

These stories are just a few happenings that have taken place in my life. As time goes by, I know my life will continue to be full of more exciting adventures that I will record later. I want my future

relatives to know all about their Aunt Shirley. These stories will show them that life is a wonderful adventure to enjoy. I want them to know that my life was "Not a Dream."

Table of Contents

The Best Parents in the World 7
The Family Picture 9
The Other Story 10
Four East Madison Street 12
The Sisters 14
Marguerite, the Oldest 16
Louise 18
My Sister Mary: (Bits, Known as Little Bits) 19
My Sister, Irene 20
Our Buddy 21
My Brother, Austin 23
My Extended Family 24
Miss Irene and Miss Pearl 26
Easter in Spain 28
Heaven on Earth 30
Grandma Griffin 33
Asthma Versus Gladys Knight 35
My Best Friend 37
What Saint Katherine of Alexandria Episcopal Church Meant
    to Me 39
Before Rosa Parks: Virginia, Not Birmingham 40
A Christmas to Remember 42
A New Experience 44
An Air Raid Drill Remembered 46
A Thanksgiving to Remember 48
Beautiful Cortina, Italy 51

An Embarrassing Moment 52
Israel 54
Crossing the Atlantic 57
Bus Duty Gone Bad 60
Determination 62
Friendship—The State of Being Friends 63
Meeting My Future In-laws: Let's Meet Charles' Family 65
My First Car—"Black Beauty" 67
My First Pair of High Heel Shoes 68
My Parents' Night Out 69
My South Sea Experience 71
My Two-Day Job 73
The Engagement Ring 75
My Wedding Day 77
Once an Actress 79
Remembering High School 81
Skipping School 83
Switzerland 85
The Bomb Scare 87
The Bravest Man I Had Ever Known 89
The Bus Trip from Hell 90
The Day Elvis Arrived at Campo Pond 93
Thought to be Algerian 94
The Egypt Adventure 96
Venezuela 99
The Penguin Parade 101
The Retreat At Happy Ours 103
The School of Horrors 105
The Table Turns 107
What a New Year Eve! 110
Valentine for a Lifetime 112
Trip to West Berlin 113
Someone once wrote: 115

The Best Parents in the World

Thomas and Louise Johnson: married for 60+ years until death parted them; raised seven children; educated through college level six children, cared for one son, Thomas, who was retarded.

My mother was a strong, kind, businesswoman. Not only did she raise her family, she owned and operated a Beauty Parlor. Working together, my parents were able to acquire two homes, one in the city and one in Anne Arundel County. My mother was very protective of her children. She wanted them near whenever possible. This carried over even as they became adults.

My father was also very protective, but in a different way. He wanted his children to experience every possible thing that would prepare them for the outside world. Although not an educated man as far as schooling was concerned, he was educated about life. Both parents knew that their children had to be educated to have a profession, not just a job. We were raised to be responsible adults.

With mother at the shop, siblings in school, and my being too young for school, I had my father to myself during the day. Since we lived where he worked, I could go on errands he had to do for the doctors. We sometimes delivered maggots and x-rays to hospitals throughout the city. Maggots were used to destroy disease in wounds. This was discovered during the First World War. (My father told me about this.) After we delivered everything, I was treated to a homemade fruit tart which were sold near the hospital.

I became very protective of my father. If my mother raised her voice to him, I would get an attitude until he took me aside and said "Your mother is my wife and she can raise her voice to me anytime she wants to."

My feelings were hurt, but it put me back in my place. (After I married, I understood my mother.)

Nothing was more important to them than their family. They would do without to make sure we had everything we needed. I am sure that there were many time they went without so that where children did not have to go without. We were taught to look out for each other. The "Golden Rule" was a very important of their life. Although we were a large family, they always shared with others.

Our childhood included picnics in Druid Hill Park, baseball games, bicycling, rollerskating, summer camp, step games, parades, free streetcar rides on Sunday, band concerts, listening to the radio, Sunday drives, and playing family games.

Attending church was a high priority. All except my father were Episcopalian. He was Methodist. He eventually joined us in his later years. We were exposed to art museums, libraries, classical music in 13 inch records, theatre and music lessons.

As we grew up and followed our paths in life, they were very proud of all of us. Although they are gone from us, we will always remember how blessed we were to have "The Best Parents in the World."

Our childhood included picnics in Druid Hill Park, baseball games, Bicycling, roller skating (indoors and outside), summer camp, step games, parades, free streetcar rides, band concerts, listening to the radio and playing family games.

Attending church was high priority. All except my father were Episcopalian. He was Methodist. He eventually joined us in his old age. We were exposed to art museums, libraries, concerts, classical music on thirteen-inch records, theatre and music lessons.

The Family Picture

In a family album there is a picture of my sisters, brother and little me at the age of five. It was a warm summer day. We were together just to enjoy each other. The picture was taken outside of our playhouse "Kitty Wink," which was two large rooms over a garage. A brownie box camera, which was one of the family's cherished items. (In those days, the only film was black and white.) The yard was a block long with trees, grass, flowers, ivy and a large birdbath. My father's job was custodian and caretaker for a large office building. We also lived there in this magical place.

My look was one of contentment. Not a worry in the world. My mother made my dress. According to one of my older sisters, it was blue with white flowers and a large white collar. I'm standing surrounded by my siblings feeling secure and loved. Although this picture was taken in the city, it felt and looked like a park. There was a wrought iron gate that was the entrance from the street. Beyond that gate was reality. Beyond that gate the "white world" that did not accept our living at 4 East Madison Street. (That's another story.)

The Other Story

It is not pleasant to remember being treated as if you are nothing. This was the way we were treated outside of the gate. Being called insulting names, not being able to sit in the square and listen to concert music unless a white person was with you. (Some of the doctors at the office that would come to take us) being chased out of the Flower Mart Festival, passing schools to get to the "colored" school, having to sit in the balcony whether you wanted to or not. (It had not been realized that they were the best seats in the house.) Not being able to go into some theatres, not able to eat in certain establishments, not being accepted in some department stores (and those that did accept you would not let you try on any thing.) And what about not being able to attend the universities in the same state? The state chose to send "colored people" out of the state at the state's expense to any university they wanted to attend. Of course, this was a good thing. The teachers went from Canada to Hawaii. The state did not change this policy until 1954. That was like closing the barn door after the horse had escaped.

Are you bored yet? An entire book could be written about the injustices we suffered because of the color of our skin and living at 4 East Madison Street. But entering that gate was a haven of peace, rest and love. You might wonder how we could handle this treatment day in and day out. Our parents made us strong. We were taught to "take our planes a little higher" and never stoop to anyone's level, no matter what. Our parents saw that we were well educated, not only in academics, but in the arts. We were taught The Golden Rule, "Do unto to others as you would have them do unto you." Being a close-knit family helped to alleviate some of the hurt.

WAS IT A DREAM

A few hours behind the gate wiped out those days' wounds, but we knew we had to go through the gate tomorrow and face it all over again.

Four East Madison Street

You read about the magic of 4 East Madison Street's yard in my essay "A Photo Essay". Well, let's go inside to see the magic through the eyes of a 5-year old.

Picture a large front door with carved designs in the wood, etched window glass and brass knobs. Open that front door and step into a large vestibule with a black and white marble floor. There is another door, the same size as the front door, decorated the same.

Enter that door and you are standing in the foyer. There is a huge mirror that takes up the entire wall and beautiful hardwood floors. A huge chandelier with 300 crystals. (I know because we had to help my father clean them.) A mahogany curved stairway with a banister that we loved to slide down.

The living room was also huge with a marble fireplace, four tall windows, couches, chairs, lamps, side tables, one long table, and beautiful window treatments. On this floor was a large room with an alcove of windows that looked out into the yard. . The secretaries worked in this room. No computers or fax machines, just typewriters, file cabinets and telephones.

The X-ray area and dressing rooms were on this floor also.

Under the stairs in an alcove was a wheelchair. (What a good time we had with that.) I still have it at my home. It is wood with large wheels and webbing upholstery. This chair can be turned into a stretcher.

There was a little self service elevator that went to the second and third floors. The doctors offices were located on these floors. Each room in this building had Oriental Rugs. There were large restrooms on each floor. They had marble floors and brass fixtures.

WAS IT A DREAM

On the second floor was the plaster room. Here the doctors made molds of the patient's feet and made plaster casts needed for different parts of the body.

After the office closed, we would slide down the banister, ride the elevator; roll around in the wheelchair and mold figures with plaster. It was magic to me. I guess you had to be there!

The Sisters

There were five of us. Two sisters were fourteen and fifteen years older than I. Therefore, I don't remember too much of them during my childhood. The other three, Bits, Irene and me were like The Three Musketeers". We did most things together. Bits was like our "second mother." My mother owned a beauty shop and worked very hard. Bits being the oldest took care of us as far as keeping us on target with what was to be done in the running of the home, our clothes and activities outside of the home.

"Mama left us money for our school clothes. When we come home from school, let's go to the Hub and pick out some pretty stuff. Hurry home so we can shop before everyone gets home."

It is amazing how styles come back into fashion. We purchased twin sweater sets, plaid skirts, plain skirts, skirts with matching vests and four pairs of penny loafers in black, navy blue, dark green and brown. In those days girls did not wear pants unless we were going on a picnic. We bought a wool jacket for each of us in different colors. Of course there was the Pea Jacket that was popular because of the war. We only got one of them because they only came in navy blue.

For some reason I will never understand, the three of us were so close to each other's size, that we exchanged everything including shoes. This gave each of us many changes of clothes. We would select things that the three of us liked and match them up with the shoes.

Each morning, we would select what we wanted to wear. We stayed sharp!! When we got home from school, Bits would make sure we prepared the clothes we had worn so they would be ready at all times. We had to shine the shoes we had worn when we took them off. (She was a tough "little mother.")

I remember on Saturday, the laundry man would bring the wet wash (the family clothes) and it was our job to hang it out to dry before my father came home at noon from work. If this was done and the home was cleaned, we would receive twenty-five cents each. Twenty-five cents was enough for the movies or we could go to the deli and buy a hot dog, chips, an orange soda and a comic book.

"Hey Daddy. We are finished all of the work. Everyone did what they were to do."

"Did you check behind Shirley? You know she tries to get out of doing her job, or did you do it?"

"No, Daddy, she even helped to hang the clothes up."

"I want my twenty-five cents like everybody else."

Daddy checks everything out. We follow him foot to foot. "It looks good. I know Mama will appreciate it when she gets home from work. Well, here is your money."

Out the door we would go.

The three of us were responsible for cleaning up after meals. That was a great time because we would harmonize as we worked. As we got older and it was time for someone to leave the nest, it was so hard on me, being the youngest. Everyone would come home on Sunday for dinner. That was a happy time for me. I had buddies again.

Marguerite, the Oldest

She was tall and stately. Being the first child, Mama was learning on her. My being the last child, Mama had learned. Marguerite was timid and I was anything but timid. Marguerite did what she was told without question. I questioned before I would do. Of course this did not sit too well with my parents. Here is an example.

"Marguerite, will you go to the store for me?"
"Yes. What do you need?"
"Shirley, will you go to the store for me?"
"Why?"

Marguerite taught the first grade for 45 years. She was happy there. Would not change for any reason. She felt secure. As a result, she was one of the best reading teachers in the system. There was not a child sent to her that she could not teach how to read.

Marguerite was a teacher in the demonstration school that was used by the teacher's college to train students. At this time the college was on the third floor of this school.

(The college now has a large campus and is a university.)

When it was my time to go to college, I went to this, as we called it, "six rooms and bath" college. Every morning I would get a lecture from my father. " Shirley, please don't do anything that would embarrass Marguerite. Remember that those teachers at the college have what you want, a degree. You are there to get that degree. Do what you are supposed to do without question."

"Now, Daddy, what could I do to embarrass Marguerite? I'm on the third floor and she is on the first."

"Oh, you'll find something. But I am warning you, if you do, you are going to be punished."

WAS IT A DREAM

Well, pinochle was the only game in town for college students in the Baltimore area. One day a group, including me, was playing Double Pinochle. We were in the room where our next class was to start. When we heard the bell. We did not stop playing since we were where we belong for our next class. I had all of the trumps. My partners were helping. I got excited. I stood up and slapped the first card on the table. By now other students were in the room and there was a loud yell. I slapped the next card on the table, but there was no yell. I turned around and there stood the president, Dean of Women and our professor.

When I saw the group, I looked at my last card, which was the ace of trumps and said, "Well, I might as well play this." I slammed it on the table. The next words I heard were, "Miss Johnson, we'll see you in the office."

When I got home, Marguerite was in the kitchen crying. Daddy and Mama were there.

"I thought I told you not to do anything that would embarrass Marguerite. I don't want to hear that you were playing cards in school."

"Daddy, everyone plays during our free time."

"Well, you don't have anymore free time. You are to study and I mean it!"

I started crying. As I was leaving the kitchen, Mama said quietly, "Did you win?"

Well, I did many things that embarrassed Marguerite, but I also did more things that made her proud. My sister crossed over this year, 2006. We miss her very much.

Louise

The quiet one, better known as "sister", was the second child in the family. She is the "jack of all trades." Sister was mother, beautician, teacher, and welder during WW2, chef and a sister I could depend one. I remember needing somewhere to live after returning from Germany. Sister moved me in with her family. At that time I was teaching at #144, which was around the corner from Sis. I could not wait to get home from school to see what we were having for dinner. It was always a surprise and very tasty.

Sister is a great grandmother now. She is still taking of her family by being there for them at all times. I was too young to remember her during my early years. but I am enjoying having her as my big sister in this stage of my life.

My Sister Mary
(Bits, Known as Little Bits)

After high school, Mary attended Coppin Teachers College, which was located on the top floor of an elementary school on Mount Street in Baltimore. She was chosen as "Miss Coppin" of 1947. We were so proud of her.

Whenever Bits had a job, even before becoming a teacher, she always shared with Irene and me. I remember the ice cream we got when she worked at Highs Ice Cream Store. I remember the "Pronto Pups" we use to get on Saturday nights.

I will never forget an outfit that Bits bought me from a dress shop named "Valentines." It was a skirt and vest set that was beige corduroy on one side and reverse to wool tweed that had green, white, tan and a tint of orange. I was so proud of the outfit that after 60+ years, I still remember it.

Mary married Scotty Gross and had three girls (Charlene, Joyce and Leslie) that became like my own. As they were growing up, I was allowed to take them everywhere I went. I enjoyed them so much.

Now that we are older, it is my turn to do for "my Bits" whatever it takes to make her happy. I hope I am doing that.

As you read on, you will read more about Mary (Little Bits).

My Sister, Irene

Irene is the 6th child in the family. She and I were close since we were the last two. We were known as "the girls" by the rest if the family. We went to school together, took piano lessons, went to the library, Sunday school at St. Mary's Episcopal Church, shopping, and spent most of our time with each other.

Irene is the sister that you will read about in my story "My Two Day Job".

As we got older, our activities were not always together, but one thing we enjoyed was going skating at the Coliseum. We were really "something else" in our skating outfits and our white roller skates. We shared this fun with our friends, Bernice and Marilyn.

Irene attended Coppin Teachers College, better known now as Coppin State University. In her last year, she was voted "Miss Coppin" (1953) which is the highest honor one could receive from the college. I was so proud of her. She was the second one in the family to receive this honor. Mary (Bits) had received it in 1947.

As life moves on, we are led in different directions, but the sisterly love will always remain.

Our Buddy

His real name was Thomas Newton Johnson Jr. Thomas was my oldest brother. He was the third child in a family of seven. As a baby, Brother, as his siblings called him, by the age of one, had all of the childhood diseases. Years ago, there was less medical knowledge than there is today. This condition left him retarded. As a mother would, she protected him. Her name for him was Buddy.

As a child, my older sisters tell me that he was very mischievous. Brother got a kick out of annoying the other children. My parents saw to it that we did not leave Brother out of anything.

"Mama, may we go to the movies?"

"If you take Buddy with you."

"Oh Mama, he sings loud in the movie theatre. Then we are put out because he will not stop."

"I repeat. If you take Buddy with you, you can go to the movies."

"Buddy, I want you to behave yourself, do you hear?"

"Yes, Mama."

They took him to the movies. (I guess Mama needed a break). He was all right until the **"Lone Rider"** came on the screen. Not only did he sing, he stood up on the seat and rode as if he was on a horse.

"Brother, get down and shut up."

"I'm the Lone Rider, the rider of the plains." He sang loud and clear.

"We're going to tell Daddy on you!"

By this time, the usher came and said they would have to leave.

As Brother got older, he got harder to handle, so the doctors suggested that he be put in Crownsville Hospital. To let him know that he was still a part of the family, our parents would pack up the Sunday dinner and we would get in the Ford for the trip to Crownsville. Back in those days, there was only one type of hospital for retarded and mental patients. This was called Crownsville State Hospital.

One day Mama gave Daddy three packages to deliver. One for me, one for Brother and one for Austin, my other brother. Daddy got mixed up and gave Brother my package.

Mama called me and said, "Is that hat what you wanted?"
"What hat?"
"The hat Daddy brought you, my Beaver hat?"
"Daddy didn't give me a hat. He gave me some cake."
"The cake was for Brother."
"Ask him where is the hat?"
"Daddy, where is the hat?"
"What hat?"
"You must have given Brother the hat. Go back and get my hat from him and give him the cake."

Well, Daddy went back to get the hat and Brother was strutting around the campus with the hat on his head.

"Brother, that hat is for Shirley. This cake is yours. You don't want to wear that. It is a women's hat. Give it to me."

"No! Mama sent this to me and I like it."

Daddy tried his best to get the hat, but nothing worked. He called my mother and told her that Brother would not give up the hat. Of course, Mama was upset.

"It was your fault, so you owe me another one."

Now, when we would go to visit Brother, winter, summer, spring or fall, he was wearing that Beaver hat.

After my parents "crossed over," Brother became my charge. This did not sit well with him because he said I was the meanest one in the family. I accepted that because it kept him straight.

Well, Brother "crossed over" December 2005 at the age of 78. He gave us a run for our money, but we really miss him.

My Brother, Austin

There is a four-years difference in our ages, therefore I don't remember much about Austin during the early years. He attended Morgan State University. There he met his wife, Doris. They had two boys. He worked at Westinghouse as a wiring supervisor until his retirement.

Austin and Doris live in Waterbury Heights, across the lawn from me. It's great to have a brother so close. Of course, I don't know how he feels about that!

"Hey Austin, can you come over here to help me? Hey Austin, I need to move this. Austin, please go with me!"

He always tries to do whatever is asked of him, not just from me, but three other sisters. He always has time for all of us. We are so blessed to have a brother that looks out for all of the family.

Austin is a faithful member of the Saint Katherine of Alexandria Episcopal Church. He helps with the upkeep of the building, attends meetings and does the church bulletins every Sunday.

In our neighborhood, he has been president of our Waterbury Heights Civic Association. He has also served on many committees.

What a guy! What would we do without him? We love him dearly.

My Extended Family

"When God closes one door, He opens another."

That quote is so true. A young family built a home near my home. They moved in at the time my husband "crossed over." I was heartbroken and had a lot of pity parties. I also had a hip replacement during that time. About a week later there came a knock at my door. There stood a young girl about 13 years old with this bubbling personality and said, "Hello. My name is Ericka. I live up there. Would you like to go to my school concert with my mother and me? I play the violin in the orchestra. We will come to get you. Are you able to walk?"

"Yes. I can walk a little if I take my time. Does your mother know that you have invited me to go? This will be my first time out in a long time."

"It will be fine. I'll tell her when I get home. We will pick you up at 6 o'clock."

Off she goes running up the hill to her home. I start getting ready. I hope that I will be able to handle this walker.

About 6 o'clock, Erick's mother came and introduced herself. She had a baby with her. She said "Hi. I'm Tina, Ericka's mother and this is Autumn. She is two months old."

"It is so nice to meet you. Autumn is so cute. Are you sure I will not be a problem to you? Ericka invited me before asking you if it would be alright."

"Oh yes. Everything is fine. We are glad you are going with us."

We enjoyed the concert. Ericka was second chair. As soon as it was over, she told her mother, "Next year I will be first chair. I'm hungry. May we go to Wendy's?"

Since that night, this family has been a joy to me. I met Lester, the father. He loves to cook, especially for picnics. His buddies are a part of all the activities. I think of them as my sons. I consider myself as a part of Tina's family and Lester's family. I am included in family activities. They have taken me to dances, picnics, house parties, school football games, theatres and graduations. Ericka had grown to be a full-fledged teenager. She would bring her boyfriends to see me. Of course, I liked the ones she didn't like. I was there when Ericka went on her first date, senior prom, and cotillion. The family's friends have become my friends.

Ericka went to college. How I missed her. Now she is 21 and lives on her own. Whenever home, she calls me. "Will you make me some chicken and rice? Do you have any bacon? I know you have some orange juice." Of course my answer is always yes.

Autumn has taken up where Ericka left off. She is 7. I take care of her after school or whenever I am asked. I look forward to watching her grow into a wonderful adult should the Lord delay His coming. I believe this meeting of the Sims family and me was meant to be.

"When God closes one door, He opens another."

Miss Irene and Miss Pearl

These ladies were my mother's best friends for at least 80 years. They were devoted sisters who lived and worked together their entire life. Where one went, the other went. Fashion was their name. They loved to look good at all times from head to toe. Miss Pearl designed clothes and hats for Miss Irene. Miss pearl designed clothes and hats for Miss Irene. New York was the place that they shopped for materials, flowers, felt and straw-hat forms, shoes, jewelry and lingerie.

"My dear, I made my sister a beautiful strapless evening gown to wear to the dance in Washington. She was the only one in a strapless dress."

Every year they walked on 5th Avenue in the Easter Parade. A few times, they were interviewed because of their BIG hat they were wearing. Of course, Miss pearl was thrilled since she made them.

"My dear, did you see us in the Easter parade? My sister got some orders for hats. She is so excited. We have to go back to New York for Pearl to design them. We are thrilled."

During the early years of their lives, there were so many things they were not allowed to do because of segregation. Miss Pearl wanted to attend a millinery school. There was no place for her to go to learn the trade. So, after attending school through the 8th grade, the sisters became maids at a doctor's home and office. The doctor's business got successful, so he made Miss Pearl his nurse assistant and Miss Irene became the receptionist. The business became 4 East Madison Orthopedic Office with six doctors. They stayed in those positions until they were forced to retire at the ages of 90 and 92.

WAS IT A DREAM

Miss Irene married Mr. Dodson. He had to move in with the sisters because they had to stay together. He preceded them in death.

Miss Irene and Miss Pearl became my "charges" until their death. In their old age, they were a hand full. They still went to all social events, church, bus trips, cruises and anything else that came up. Money was not a problem for them. They enjoyed giving it away to people who were down and out. Supporting their church was top priority. Miss Irene loved to cruise, so I had to go with her each time. If they went on a bus trip, I had to go with them to assist them.

Miss Irene died at the age of 95 in 1993. Miss Pearl died at the age of 101 in 1997. I really miss the Johnson Sisters.

Easter in Spain

"Easter will be here soon. Where are we going?"

"Elaine suggested Spain. She said that they have a Parade of Silence and she would like to see what it is like."

"Sounds good to me. We will have to fly. See when everyone can leave."

"Paul said they were going before us, but will meet us at the airport there."

I did not know that a joke was going to be played on me until we got to the airport in Spain. As I got off of the plane, Paul and the fellows that were with him came rushing to me with a large bunch of flowers and yelling, "She's finally here! We welcome you to Madrid. Please come this way. You car is waiting."

I was so shocked. They were strangers gathering around me trying to see who this was. When we got into the car, they just fell out laughing.

We checked in to the hotel. Sarah was a Coca Cola freak. She drank a Coke every morning as soon as she woke up. As soon as we registered, she asked, "Please have a coke brought to my room every morning."

"The clerk said Coca Cola is not sold in Spain."

"Well, I will have to have a Coke, so I'm going back to Germany."

"You mean to tell us that you can't give up Coke for a week?"

"I'm going home!"

So she went home. We toured the city. As soon as the sun went down, all of the cars, buses, bikes, etc. were nowhere to be seen. The street was completely quiet. No one talked. When the Parade of

Silence started, there was not a sound. The parade had the Twelve Stations of the Cross on flatbed trucks with people posing as the statues on the stations on the wall of churches. Behind them came people dressed in shrouds dragging a ball and chain on their ankles: they were the ones who felt they had sinned. This was their way of atonement. This went on until dawn of Easter.

The next day we went to see the bull fight. I never want to see that again. I love animals. To see them tortured was too much for me. I started rooting for the bull. That did not sit too well with the natives.

After a few days of flamenco dancing we returned home a little more educated about the Parade of Silence.

Heaven on Earth

It was 1962 when Charles and I decided to have our home built. We decided on a Ranch house with basement. That was a popular style during that time. We found some land, but it was too small for the house.

Charles was working on the night shift. The builder called and said "Mrs. Griffin, I have found the perfect land for your house."

"Where is it located"?

"It's in an area called Waterbury Heights. We must move fast because it is an excellent price and will go fast."

"Charles is at work. We will have to wait until tomorrow."

"That will be too late. We must go to see it now."

I decided to go without Charles. The builder and I went to see the land. (I failed to tell you that it was nighttime.) Using a huge spotlight, we proceeded to walk the perimeter of the land. It was an acre and a half. The cost was $1100.00. (Who could turn that down?)

The next morning, instead of going to school, I went to purchase the land. (No, I didn't mention this to Charles.) When I got to the office, there was a man, Mr. Foxwell, who owned the entire Waterbury Heights area.

I said, "I'm here to purchase lot #1 in Waterbury Heights."

"That lot is $1100. You only have to put down $15.00 and $15.00 a month."

"I'm here to pay all of the $1100 today."

"You can't do that. All your people pay a little at a time."

"I am going to pay all of it today! I have nothing to do with what other people do."

This did not sit well with Mr. Fowwell! I found out later that he made money by foreclosing on the lots if someone missed one payment.

On the weekend, I took Charles to see what I had purchased. Well, in the light, everything looked very different. It had rained the night before and the little dirt road was a muddy path. We had to walk to our lot or what I thought was our lot. I could really see the "woods" I had purchased. I thought Charles was going to have a heart attack.

"What were you thinking about"? (Of course my tears began to flow.)

"I could not see it too well."

"Well, that should have told you something I can't believe that you bought land sight unseen."

"Gilbert (the builder) said that it was a great piece of land, so I took him at his word" (Tears still flowing)

"Well, let's go see what Gilbert has in mind. Stop crying. At least we own woods." (I knew I had won. Tears will do it every time.)

The building started. I went every day to watch. Each night I read books about building a house. I would ask questions and the workmen thought I knew what I was talking about. It kept them on their toes. I did not know a thing!

In 120 days, my house was complete. We were elated. We named it "Happy Ours." Charles was still on night shift, so my mother and father helped me move in. When it was time for them to go, my mother did not want to leave me down here in the dark. Believe me, it was dark! You could not see your hands before your face. My father said, "Weez, (that is what he called her) we are not staying any longer. Shirley will be fine."

Through her tears, she said, "If you were any kind of father, you would not want to leave her here in God-forsaken place alone."

"Well you know I'm not any kind of father, I'm a good father! This is her home and she will be fine."

I assured her that Charles would be home in an hour.

After a few years, we had quite a few neighbors. Everything went well. We both felt that all of this was not given just for us, but to share with others. To meet that end, we shared our home with groups of Senior Citizens, Bible Study groups, retreats, schools, our neighborhood, family and friends for picnics and parties. We knew it was the right thing to do because for 40+ years, it never rained on "OUR PARADE!" We never had to have a rain date.

It is believed that I have a DLTG (Direct Line To God).

Grandma Griffin

Being introduced to Helen Griffin was a real experience. When Charles and I decided to get married, he wanted me to meet his father's mother. This would also give me an opportunity to meet his father who was dying of cancer.

When we arrived at the house on that cold November day, I was greeted with a hug. We went upstairs to see Charles's father. After a short visit, we all went downstairs. Miss Helen asked Charles to go to the drugstore for her. She said the two of us could talk while he was gone.

As soon as the front door closed, she said, "Get out of my house" She opened the door and pushed me out into the cold. Then she threw my coat out to me and said, "Don't come back here again and leave my grandson alone!"

I did not know what had happened. When Charles returned, I was sitting on the steps, crying. He could not believe that his grandmother would do such a thing. When questioned, she said, "She is nothing but a whore. You get rid of her."

He got in the car and was very apologetic. I was determined to make her like me because he really loved her.

His father died. I found out that Miss Helen had been so mean to people, including her daughter in law that no one wanted to be around her. My mother (bless her heart) made our family go to the funeral so that someone would be there for Charles. Some of my friends and my Godmother came also.

Not long after that, Miss Helen became ill. We would put her in the hospital and she would check herself out. The last time she did that, the hospital refused to accept her. Her condition was very bad. My mother (bless her heart again) went to look after her because Charles and I were working.

My mother called and said, "Miss Helen wants to see you".

"I don't want to see her."

"But Shirley, she is dying. She probably wants to make up with you."

"OK, I'll be there as soon as I can."

I decided to take some flowers. When I arrived, Miss Helen asked everyone to leave the room. She wanted to talk to her "granddaughter." (I should have started running then.")

I went to her bed. She pulled me close to her mouth and said, "You leave my grandson alone. You get out of my house. You are nothing but a whore after my money." I ran out of the house and went home without saying anything to anyone. When I walked in my door, the phone was ringing. It was my mother. Miss Helen had died.

Asthma Versus Gladys Knight

"Charles, I got our tickets to see Gladys Knight at Pier One next Saturday Night. I am so excited."

"I know. You think no one can sing but her. Where are the seats located?"

"They are on the front row, right where she will be standing. I asked for those seats and got them. What am I going to wear?"

I had been trying to get rid of my asthma for about a week. It seemed worse every day. I went to school and taught all of my classes, but I was feeling worse. When I made my way home around 4:30, I could not get in the door without the help of Charles. He knew I was very sick and called 911. I passed out in the dining room. The last thing I remember saying was, "Charles, please take care of me."

When I woke up, I was in the hospital on a respirator. I could see that it was 11:30 pm. The nurse came to me and said that I would be in the hospital until Monday. My doctor wanted me to get some rest.

"I have to go home tomorrow because I go to see Gladys Knight in concert Saturday night. I feel fine. There is no way that I can stay here and miss that. Please call my doctor and tell her I need to go home."

"Shirley, you had better listen to the doctor and forget about the concert."

"Now Charles, you know better than that. I feel fine and I am going to the concert."

The nurse returned and said that my doctor said she would not sign for me to leave the hospital until Monday.

"I will sign myself out tomorrow."

I signed myself out against everyone's wishes, went home, got sharp and went to the concert. My seat was directly in front of Gladys and the mike. I had a wonderful time. There were no after-effects from my actions. I have decided when I grow up; I'm going to be just like Gladys!

My Best Friend

It was 1944, the first day of junior high school when God looked down and saw a little girl sitting alone, looking very serious. In the room was another little girl who was laughing and enjoying herself.

God said, "Those two need to meet. They will be good for each other."

So, somehow Shirley Johnson met Constance Tate. Connie, as she was called, was serious about life. Shirley was anything but serious. They became very good friends. It was a very unusual friendship because they did not hang out together, but they were always there for each other.

They went to the same college to become teachers. They had their first assignment at the same school. They got their cars the same year. They even approved each other's husbands to be.

I retired after 30 years of teaching. Connie had become a principal a few years before. Retiring was one thing we did not do together. I begged her to retire with me so that we could travel before we got too old. She wanted to stay a few more years at this school.

In 1990, Connie retired. I spoke at her retirement party. We spent more time together doing things with our husbands. We went on a cruise to the Mediterranean for 23 days. When we returned, Connie became ill. She passed away January 1996. It hurts to lose your best friend. How I wish we could have had more time to share our old age.

I found this reading that shows the kind of friend she was to me.
"This was my friend,
The first to offer praise when I found success to crown my days,
And when I was afraid or failed or grieved.

SHIRLEY JOHNSON GRIFFIN

The first to reach my side, the last to leave.
This was my friend,
Who saw my lonely task and helped me by some thoughtful deed
Before I even asked; with her, there was no reason to pretend.
She knew my faults and loved me anyway. My Friend."
Unknown

What Saint Katherine of Alexandria Episcopal Church Meant to Me

As a child, living at 506 Bloom Street, St. K's was the church that I learned about being a good Episcopalian. I was taught by Sisters who made sure I understood the rules for conduct in the church; no talking, when to genuflect, when to stand and when to kneel, when to make the sign of the cross, the seriousness of communion, etc.

We also had to learn the catechism verbatim. The Sisters asked the questions and we had better know the answers! After learning this, you were rewarded at the age of 12 to dress up in all white from head to toe. The Bishop would come on a special Sunday service. We would go to him one at a time. He would put his hands on our head and say

"Defend, Oh Lord, this child with thy Heavenly Grace, that she may continue to be Thine forever and daily increase in thy Holy Spirit more and more until Thy coming Again."

That early learning has kept me in good stead as I go through this journey. I am quite a few years from childhood, but I still remember how I got started. My life has been and still continues to be such a joy.

My testimony is "God always changes my struggles into blessings."

It all started at Saint.Katherine of Alexandria Episcopal Church.

Before Rosa Parks
Virginia, Not Birmingham

June 27th, 1954. That was the date of my brother's wedding that was being held in Hampton, VA. The family drove down for this special day. Doris, the bride to-be looked radiant. The nuptials and reception went very well. Everything was fine until it was time for me to head back home, alone, by bus.

My father drove me to the station. The passengers began boarding the bus. When it was my turn, the driver blocked my way and let the white passengers on ahead of me. When I finally got on, I sat in the seat right behind the driver. All other black people went to the back of the bus.

The driver came aboard and said, "Go to the back of the bus (N word))."

I refused to move. He continued to tell me, "(N word) are to sit in the back." I ignored him until he said, "This is why I hate (N word) to come down here. They always try to start trouble."

I finally had enough, so I said, "If you can read, and I doubt that you can, get an unabridged dictionary and look up the word (N). It will say anyone who acts contrary to good social behavior. Now who is the (N)?"

This infuriated him and he went to get the bus dispatcher, who wanted to know, "What's the holdup out here?"

(My father wanted to know also. He knew if it had anything to do with civil liberties, I had to be the cause. I had become very militant.) The driver pointed to me. The dispatcher said, "This bus will not move until you get to the back of the bus."

"I have to be back at school by September, so you can take all of the time you want."

My father tried to board the bus, but was blocked. After a few more words to me, the bus left for Richmond, VA.

There was a stopover or rest stop for the passengers. I really needed a "rest stop," but as I prepared to get off, a white lady came to me and said, "If you get off of this bus, he will leave you."

I told her I had to go to the ladies room. She said for me to wait and she would be back to help me. I had no idea what she meant, but I stayed on the bus. When the lady returned, she had an institutional size empty can. She blocked the door while I relieved myself and she proceeded to remove the can from the bus. I told her how grateful I was and thanked her profusely.

When the time was up, the bus driver jumped on the bus. When he saw me sitting there, he had some more words to say. When I reached Baltimore, I registered a complaint to the bus company. I received a letter of apology. (Too little, too late!)

You might wonder why I stood up to that situation. Why was I not afraid of going to jail? At the beginning of the story, I said it was June 27th. 1954. That was the year that it became illegal for any segregation on interstate travel. (And you thought I was just brave!)

A Christmas to Remember

Being away from home at Christmas is not an easy thing to do. I had never been away this time of the year. This year I am in Hanau, Germany, many miles from home. The friends with whom I worked and traveled had a meeting to decide what we could do to for the holidays. We agreed that we would ride the train to Austria and leave the train at the first town the train stopped. When either of us felt homesick, we would catch the train and go to another country. We would do this until our vacation was over.

Our first stop was in a quaint little village named Vargron. We took the only cab in the town to the village, which was located high up on a mountain. When we arrived the entire town had turned out for our arrival. We were so surprised. We found out later that if the train stops there, the town knows someone is coming.

The people were dressed in their style of dress. The band played and people pulled us into a dance. (It was cold, but we cooperated.) The English language was not spoken there so there was not any conversation. We pointed, smiled and shook our heads. We were taken to the home where we stayed. It was small with two bedrooms. Each had two beds in each room. The room was very bright with colorful spreads and curtains. The bathroom was small with toilet and washbasin.

At dinner we were give a roasted cauliflower with a sprinkle of cheese on top. The custom there was to fast on Christmas Eve. After the midnight mass, there would be a great feast. Our sign language worked very well. We were starved but we went along with the program. (We had to. There was no food to be found.)

At midnight we were taken further up the mountain in cable cars. What a beautiful sight! The moon and stars felt so close. You could almost touch them. There was snow on the mountain. With the moon shining on it made the town look like something out of a fairy tale. The closer we go to the top of the mountain the more you could hear a bugle playing "Silent Night." It brought tears to our eyes.

We finally reached this beautiful church inside and outside. We had special seats. Everyone either shook our hands or curtsied. There was no heat in the church. We almost froze. The ladies of the town had furs like we had never seen before. They wore the entire animal the head, tail and body. It was something to see. We were so cold by the time the service was over, we felt like going to sleep. The ride down the mountain could not go fast enough. We were fed a wonderful meal. We had no idea what it was, but it was good.

On Christmas Day we exchanged gifts among ourselves. Then the missing home set in. As we had planned, we caught the next train out and went to Cortina, Italy.

That's another story!

A New Experience

An artist girlfriend of my niece asked me to tape my experiences I had in Europe. I was elated to think someone was interested. When I finished, I sent the tapes to her. After listening, she wanted to paint oil murals of some of my experiences.

I was elated when she asked me if I would pose for some pictures. Of course the answer was yes, yes, yes! My niece was going to pose also.

Our first assignment was on a replica of the Orient Express train. We had to dress as the proper ladies would have dressed in those days. This idea came from a train trip I talked about. That day, 265 photos were taken. I could not understand what she would do with the photos, but what do I know?

The next set of photos was taken on a very cold night at an area that looked like I was trying to cross a border. This idea came about when I was stopped at the border between Czechoslovakia and Germany. There was a man dressed like a border guard and a foreign car. I was dressed in a fur coat, showing my passport. My niece was in the car looking fearful.

A few weeks later, we dressed in evening clothes and went to the Lyric Theatre. The theatre was closed except for this activity. This pose included my niece, her husband and me. We were seated in the box seats. (I will tell about my experience in a theatre in East Berlin at another time.) This was the end of my posing.

About three months later, I was invited to a showing of these murals. I could not believe my eyes. There we were as big as life on display. Each mural had a wall of its own. Altogether there were five of them. The artist had painted from the photos on to canvas.

WAS IT A DREAM

Years ago, there was a theatre downtown that would not allow my people to enter. Would you believe that now, 2006, the mural that was taken in the Lyric Theatre is hanging on a wall in this downtown theatre? Oh, how times have changed!

An Air Raid Drill Remembered

In the early sixties, all of the schools had to practice Air Raid Drills. The procedure was to be discussed with your class to make them aware of what was expected of us. The procedure was at the sounding of the alarm; the teacher was to direct the children to get under their desk. There should be no talking. After the all clear sounded each class was to have a discussion. "Who can tell us why we practice air raid drill at school? Yes, Reggie. "Well, I think we do it because one day we are going to be bombed and die."

"Now, Reggie please don't say that. Who else has an idea? Robert."

"My mother said I was to come home when I heard a bomb."

"Children, PLEASE. We are not going to be bombed! Nicole."

"If we are not going to be bombed, why do we practice"?

Just as I was losing my cool, the dismissal bell sounded. "We will finish our discussion tomorrow. Please have some better ideas."

There is another drill we had to do also. The Fire Drill. This procedure was when the alarm sounded, the teacher was to line the class up and as quickly as possible and proceed to the school yard to the designated place. There was to be no talking. When the fire chief sounded the all clear, we were to return to our classroom for a discussion.

Well, one day, all of the teachers on my floor came to school wearing black. I had a feeling this was not going to be my best day. After lunch, everything was going well when an alarm went off.

I lined my class up and headed for our spot in the yard. One child kept calling my name. "You are not supposed to be talking!"

The other teachers followed my lead. We lined up in the yard as we were supposed to do.

Where were the other classes from the first and second floors? There was something wrong! The alarm was for an Air Raid Drill. We quickly got back to our rooms, but it was too late. The principal had seen us. Up to the third floor she came.

"What was that all about?

"I got confused and lead the classes to the yard."

"Have you had your discussions with the class?"

Before I could answer, one of the children said,

"I tried to tell her but she would not listen!"

The principal went back to office and announced over the intercom, "The entire third floor was wiped out today during the air raid drill. They all went to the yard. Now I know why they were all dressed in black. There will be a minute of silence. The third floor fearless leader, Shirley Johnson Griffin, led them."

A Thanksgiving to Remember

Thanksgiving was in a couple of days and my friends and I did not want to stay in Hanau for the holiday.

Rosalee said "Let's go on a bus trip to Prague, Czechoslovakia. We will be doing something and not get homesick"

We all agreed. We knew it was under communist rule, but we needed some adventure. When we got on the bus, there were some people from Voice of America, the radio station for the Americans in Europe.

The trip there was very uneventful. When we got to the border of Prague, a soldier boarded the bus. We all got excited. Some action was going to start.

He said, "Welcome to my homeland. There are 32 of you. You must stay together at all times." On the way to the hotel we had a lecture about Prague. The bus took us by a large church. We noticed that there were many brides and grooms standing in a long line outside of the church. As one couple came out of the church, the bride would hand a bunch of flowers to the next bride and that couple went in. In about 5 minutes, that couple would come out and pass the flowers to the next bride in line.

When the guard was questioned about it. He told us that Wednesday was the only day that the couples could get married. Of course, we were shocked.

As the tour progressed we were taken for a walk to see more of the city. The Voice of America people said, "We are going to break away from the group. Do you all want to go with us?"

"Yes, said Rosalee, we want to go."

As the group walked straight ahead, our group turned the corner. Little did we know that soldiers were following the entire group. Someone looked back and discovered two soldiers following us.

"Let go into this hotel bar and see if they come in there."

The group went into the bar and we sat at a table. The soldiers did not come in. We began to relax.

The waiter came to our table and asked, "Would you mind moving to a more comfortable table?" Of course we did not mind. After the drinks were ordered, we were making conversation when a drunk Czechoslovakian came to the table.

In perfect English, he asked if he could join us. While he sat with us he began to talk negatively about his country.

He said, "I am 21 years old. I am a student. My father is a professor at the university. We have no freedom here like you have in America. My father joined the communist party so he could continue receiving books. Why did you come to this place? If you get home, you stay home. This is no place for you. He began singing "God Bless America." No one in the bar seemed to pay much attention.

When we got ready to go, we did not know how to get back to our hotel, so the fellow walked back with us. When he said goodbye to us, he had tears in his eyes. We went inside and the soldiers escorted us to our rooms.

The next morning was Thanksgiving Day at home. How we longed for that dinner!

Our guide said "Today you will shop. You will stay together at all times. When we go back to the hotel, you will have an American Thanksgiving Dinner." Did our eyes brighten up! When we got to the store all of the other shoppers were put out until we left. They just stood outside and waited. Visualize this: Twenty women shopping together in a store that had very little to buy, being followed by soldiers with zip guns on their shoulders. The men were in the group also, but they had to follow us.

I think since I was the only one of color in the group, I was an easy target. I say that because an old man sidled up to me and said "why are you here? Be careful. Go home!"

When we went back to the hotel, as I was walking to the door, the fellow from the bar sided up to me and said, "The table where you were seated was bugged. Everything I said was recorded. I will not get home again. Tell your friends goodbye for me and please go home." I related the conversation to the Voice of America group. They said when they got back to their base, they will check to see if he was killed.

Well, we went to the dinner that was promised to us. When I saw it, I could have cried. We were given a hunk of cold turkey breast, a bottle of water and three apricots.

Now it is time for us to go back to Germany. We were glad to be going home. When we got to the border, we were stopped. The driver was taken off of the bus. We were kept in that cold bus for two hours. We decided to get off of the bus for a while. When we got off, the floodlights came on and there were soldiers in a tower with guns pointing at us.

Did we get back on? NO! We sat on the guardrail and sang as loud as we could, "God Bless America." They finally let the driver out. He happened to have a Czechoslovakian name and they thought he was trying to escape. They took all of his money and his coat. Well, we finally got back home. We all agreed we had our adventure.

P.S. The Voice of America called three months after we returned. Our friend had been killed.

P.S.S. You do a lot of dumb, crazy things when you are 26!

Beautiful Cortina, Italy

After leaving Austria, we caught the train to Italy. The first town reached was Cortina. The train tracks ran above the town around the edge of the mountains. The mountains surrounded the town. The town was in a valley. The mountains were covered with snow. There were aqua lights shining on the snow all the way around the town. The sight took our breath away. We had never seen anything that beautiful. A cab took us to the hotel. We could look out and see the aqua color snow and people skiing. There was an Olympic ice skating rink that made one wish they were a skater. We were told that the Olympics were held here.

The next day we walked around the town. The people were so friendly. We decided to go skiing. That was something to see. We were on the ground more than up on the skis. It was a lot of fun. We rode the lift up the slope with our skis. We were going to ski down like the others were doing.

I said, "If they can do it we can too. Let's show them how it's done."

We got off of the lift, looked down the slopes and changed our minds.

A cup of hot beverage was all we could handle. After a few more hours we decided to see when the train would come. It was time to go.

The stationmaster said, "It will be here in two hours."

That gave us time to decide we would go to Switzerland. We said goodbye to this fairy tale town.

An Embarrassing Moment

How many of you can relate to a "Bad Hair Day?" You will understand why I did what I did. I was desperate!

Teaching Physical Education did not help my situation because my hair was always disarranged. When I saw an ad in the newspaper that a department store was selling wigs, I was elated. This was an answer to a prayer.

After school, I went to see about purchasing one. It was so much fun trying on different styles and colors. After some time, I decided on one that looked like my hair. (I did not want to be too obvious.)

The next morning, I plaited my hair and put on my "new hair." For the first time, I would look good all day at school. Some co-workers knew there was something different about me, but were too polite to question me.

As the day moved on, a few peeks in the mirror let me know that I was still "sharp!" My first grade class came to the gym after lunch. They were very excited about a new dance they had seen called "The Twist." One boy had the record with him.

"Mrs. Griffin, may we do "The Twist?"

"Why, yes. We can use it for our warm-up."

Well, I started the music.

"Let's go forward, back, forward, back down, up, down up."

After doing this routine a few times, I decided we should go down, backward and up. This was not a good thing. When I went down, backward and up, my wig did not come up with me. I came up with a new hairstyle. The first-graders were flabbergasted! They were frozen in position, looking straight at me. I snatched up my wig and went behind the piano to put it on. As I looked up, there was the entire class behind the piano with me. The looks were scared, shocked, and some were ready to cry. One of the boys said, "Oh look. She's got two hairs".

I did not know whether to laugh or ignore the fiasco. The class just continued what they were doing. I was very grateful to them. They did not laugh, but their teacher did!

Israel

Have you ever read, discussed, reviewed pictures of places and things and wished you would someday see them for yourself? Well, this is about how a wish of mine came true.

It all started long ago when my siblings and I were introduced to the Bible. We heard wonderful stories of the Old and New Testaments. We saw pictures of places, people and events during those times. We were told that some of the places were still there. We could experience the wonders about which we had heard.

With a church group, the opportunity came for me to go to Israel. Preparing for a trip of a lifetime was exciting. Traveling was not new to me, but this trip was an answer to a prayer. We traveled by an Israeli Airline to Jerusalem. When we got to the Israeli terminal, we were stopped at the door. The guard there said, "Please show your passport. Go straight to line 4. There you will answer questions."

A few weeks before we left home, we had to fill out a questionnaire about our background. At line 4, we were asked, "What is your name?"

"Shirley Griffin."

"What is your mother's maiden name?"

"Tolbert."

"Did you pack your own luggage?"

"Yes."

"Did anyone give you anything like a package or letter to take with you?"

"No."

"You may enter the sitting area. Do not leave your bags unattended. If it is left alone, it will be confiscated." We finally boarded the plane for Israel.

For the next nine days we went to many of the places about which we had read. We relived the Upper Room experience. We walked the path that Jesus walked to be crucified. We saw the tomb where he was laid. On the door was a sign, "HE IS NOT HERE. HE IS RISEN."

How can I explain the emotions that were felt at that time? Some people were crying, some just walked away in wonder. It is something that must be experienced for oneself. Many groups were there. Tears flowed freely. Strangers were consoling each other. We sang and prayed.

In the planning of this trip, some of the people wanted to be baptized in the Jordan River. Although many of us had been baptized as children and young adults, we wanted the experience of the Jordan River.

The minister explained, "You can be baptized only once, but you can be immersed in the Jordan."

We all chose to be immersed, all 25 of us. The water was very cold since it was February and it was raining. The flow of the river was somewhat calm. We were all dressed in our bathing suits with white robes over the top. Each person went in alone with the minister. I felt sorry for the minister because he was in the water for such a long time. That did not bother him in the least. He was in the spirit. Each time he immersed someone, he said, "I immerse you in the name of the Father, Son, and the Holy Spirit."

Some of the people came up praising the Lord, some were crying, other were quietly in prayer.

I had suffered with asthma since I was 15 years old. At this time, I was having an attack .My roommate said" As sick as you are, you do not need to get in that cold water."

I said, "I want to be immersed and take my chances. I want to claim my healing of asthma." As I went in I prayed that God would grant me a healing.

That was the most moving experience I had ever had.

After returning home, I was very sick with an attack for five days. That attack was the last one I suffered. That was in 1989. I know my prayers have been answered.

There are some people and even some doctors who do not believe. (That sounds like a personal problem to me!) I know what happened! This is a trip that will always be remembered. I returned to Israel two other times just to relive the experience: each trip revealed something I did not see before. Now when I read the Bible or see something on TV, I can relate.

Crossing the Atlantic

"Mama, Daddy, I put in an application to teach in Europe."

"Now, I know you are crazy if you think I'm going to let you go that far away from home by yourself."

"Now, Weezie, let's hear what she has to say before we tell her no."

(Now remember, I am 26 years old.)

"I want to see the world and this is a start. The government will pay for transportation over and back. Living quarters are also provided. I have to feed myself. I will be teaching a fourth grade. I will be able to travel."

"Who are you going with?"

"No one. I have asked, but everyone has his or her own plans. I really don't need anyone to go with me."

"Weezie, I think this would be good for her to be on her own. It will make her grow up and I think she is going to go whether we want her to go or not. So, let's give her our blessings. She will be all right."

"As I always have said, you will let this child do anything she wants to do. When the time comes, she is going to change her mind."

My sister, who was very good in art, made 12 bulletin board layouts for me to take. I was so grateful. My art skills are next to nothing. I was really getting things in order. Then it happened. I almost did change my mind. Charles showed up.

We had been in high school together and had not seen each other since. We had a few dates. I told him I would be going to Europe in a few weeks. He said, "I don't want you to go. I want you to marry me."

"I have to go. I have accepted the position. I want to go. If you want to marry me when I return, I will marry you. This is something I have to do for me."

My father went to New York with me to be checked in. When the ship pulled out, I saw my Daddy wipe his eyes. That is when I wished I were not going. I was the only teacher of color on the ship. By the time we got out into the Atlantic, I had many friends.

Crossing the Atlantic was a real adventure for me. I sailed on an army transport ship, The USS Darby. We were told it would take five days to reach Bramerhaven, Germany. About two days out, the captain said, "We will be coming into bad weather. Please follow all instructions given to you by your stewards. The water will be very rough. We are taking precautions for your safety."

All of the troops were in the lower part of the ship. The other passengers were on the upper decks. As the weather got progressively worse, ropes were put up along the halls. We had to hold on to keep from falling. All of the portholes in the cabins were covered. In the dining room, we were given a plate, a cup and a spoon. The ship was rocking side to side. Every once and awhile, our steward would say "Lift, down, lift, down."

Every time he gave a command, we would lift the plate and cup. When the ship settled down. We would put them down. The only way one could see outside was when you walked pass a door that looked out on the decks. I happened to look out and the waves were taller than the ship. I had never seen anything like it.

At night we were strapped in our beds to keep from falling out. The ship rolled back and forth and side to side. Many, many people got sick. I have a strong stomach. I did not miss a meal.

It took the ship eight days to get to Germany. When we arrived, we had to find out where we would be teaching. It finally became my turn. "Good morning. My name is Shirley Johnson. I am here for an elementary grade."

"May I see your teaching certificate?"

"I don't have a teaching certificate."

"You mean you are over here without all of the papers you are supposed to have? You will have to return to the states."

My heart fell. I had never heard of a teaching certificate. While I was sitting outside of the office wondering what to do, the superintendent came and asked, "What is the problem?"

"I was told that I could not teach here because I do not have a teaching certificate. I have never had a teaching certificate."

"Where do you live in the states?"

"Baltimore, Maryland."

"What college did you attend?"

"Coppin Teachers College."

He went through some papers and said, "You do not need a certificate. That college demands 128 education credits before you can graduate. That is more than any other teachers college in the states. You do not need a certificate. We are glad to have you."

I was so relieved that I could have cried. I was finally an official member of the United States Teaching Corps.

Bus Duty Gone Bad

At the school in Germany, I had a wonderful class of children from the states and other countries. I was the only person in the room that did not speak two or more languages. These children had experiences that you would not believe. I had such a good relationship with them. I looked forward to each day.

For a week, each teacher had bus duty. This was my week. I met each bus and made sure the children entered the school. A new boy and his mother got off of the bus.

"Where is the fourth grade?"

"It's room 12. Is he in the fourth grade?"

No answer. The mother pushed aside and went into the school. When the last bus was emptied, I went into my room. There sat the parent and the boy.

"I hope you are not my boy's teacher. I don't want no (N) teaching my boy."

"You will not have any (N) teaching your boy. I am the teacher in this room."

"Well, I don't want you to teach him. Where is the principal's office?"

"I will take you to her."

"Mrs. Phillips, this parent has something to say."

"I don't want any (N) to teach my child."

"What is your name?"

"It's Mrs. Anthony Pickett."

"What is your husband's unit?"

I don't remember what she said, but Mrs. Phillips made a call. The next thing I knew, Sgt. Pickett and his commander were in the office.

"Mrs. Pickett, say what you said to me."

"I said I don't want any (N) to teach my child."

The Sgt. Said, "Betty, don't say that. Please don't say that."

The commander said, "Sgt. Phillips you are responsible for the actions of your family. Because of the attitude of your wife, you will be shipped back to the states immediately."

"But we just arrived yesterday. Please Betty, tell them you did not mean that"

"It is too late. You and your family will be shipped home. Miss Johnson, on behalf of the US Army, I want to apologize for this incident. Please accept our apology."

The husband was so upset, he was crying, "You have ruined my chance for promotion."

I felt so sorry for him. I told Mrs. Phillips I felt that she should be forgiven so as not to ruin his career.

"We are all over here representing the US. They do not tolerate any incidents of that sort."

So much lost!

Determination

"Take such lifeless musical instruments as the flute or the harp. How will anyone know the tune that is being played unless the notes are sounded distinctly?" (1 Corinthians 14:7)

Music is like fresh air to me. My ears seem to record any tune played. There was a piano in our living room, which was a magnet that drew me to it. My fingers could pick out any tune the ears heard.

At an early age, my parents recognized my talent and immediately got a teacher to give lessons to me. That did not last long because I did not want to learn the notes. I just wanted to play the piano.

After being drummed out of a Music Conservatory for not reading notes and for being a "colored child who had talent, but it would never amount to anything," I decided to do it my way. I would listen to music and practice the tunes. As a youngster, I never had a problem with self-esteem, so being able to perform to an audience was right down my alley. I played at church talent shows, showed off for company at home and would play for anyone else who would listen.

Nothing holds a child's attention for long. The piano was of no interest to me anymore. The organ was the thing! To my delight, my father purchased a chord organ for me.

From that experience, I taught myself to play the Hammond Organ. Playing for church was the greatest "high" I could possibly get. Now, at the age of 73, entertaining myself on my Hammond Organ in my home is still my favorite thing.

I learned that when you have a God-Given talent, you need no one but Him.

Friendship—The State of Being Friends

That is the definition in the Webster's Dictionary. After many years of living I have found that there are different stages of friendship. The first friendship that is developed is with your family. You learn to share, love, look out for each other, fuss, make up and support each other when necessary. Somewhere in all of that you form friendships.

Then, it's time to go to school. You meet a lot of children. Somewhere in the crowd, you meet someone who is a little special. Both of you seem to click. When you get home, you say "Mama I met Rita today. She likes to do things I like to do . We are best friends."

As we move along in life, we hold on to some friendships and some we lose for different reasons. At this stage of my life, most of my friends are women who have been in my life for 40+ years. I have been blessed with friends who support each other in all situations.

Somewhere I have read that you are blessed if you find four good friends during your lifetime. I thank God that this statement was not true for me. I truly have a lot of close friends. It is so true that to have friends, you must be a friend. I love being around my friends. I love doing things for my friends.

I must share with you this story about the closeness of friends (Rosie, Gerri, Shirley).

"Shirley, I am going to take the exam to become a principal next week. Gerri is also going to take it after which we are going to dinner. Do you want to meet us for dinner?"

"Why can't I take the test with both of you?"

"You don't want to be a principal."

"I know, but I will take it to give both of you moral support. Sign me up and get my entrance pass.

"But you haven't even studied."

"I don't care. You just sign me up. Where are we going to dinner?"

We took the test and we all passed. Rosie and Gerri got promoted. I went back to the gym. That's friendship!

Friends are God's way of taking care of us. One Friend might be good during sad times. Another might like traveling with you. I have friends who love to go to concerts and plays. Others just want to be intellectual and keep the group on top of things. I like to cook big meals for my friends and enjoy watching them enjoy.

Some friends you do not see for years, but when you do meet again, it is just like you never left each other. So friendship is a love for special people in your life.

Meeting My Future In-laws
Let's Meet Charles' Family

Virginia (Mother) better known as Dee Dee; Monroe Sr. (Father), Monroe Jr. (better known as Money), Virginia (Sister) better known as Baby Sis, Dorothy (Aunt) better known as Dimp, Ellen (aunt), Seawood (uncle) better known as Woodie.

This was the family of my fiancé. They all lived in Elkridge on Taylor's Hill. The three homes are a hop, skip and jump from each other. Charles took me to meet everyone at his mother's home. We gathered in the living room I was a little nervous. Dee Dee said,

"Shirley, I understand you teach school."

"Yes, I teach the fourth grade."

"Oh, that is what Monroe is going to do. He is going in to practice next week. Tell him something that will help him."

(In my circle of friends, I'm known as "Motor Mouth." I start talking and can't stop.)

I started, "You must get control of your class first. You cannot accomplish anything if you do not have control. Here's an example: There was a Participation Class next door to me. The Senior Teacher left two students in charge of the class while she went to a meeting. There was so much noise in the room that I went in to see what was wrong. As I entered the door, there was a real tall man (I got up and proceeded to demonstrate how tall) blocking the door. I went in the room and there was this big fat man (I proceeded to again demonstrate how big and fat) sitting on some children trying to hold them in their seats."

At this point, Money said "Was that at school 112?"
"Yes."
"Well, the big fat man was me."

Well, the room went wild with laughter. Dee Dee laid out on the floor, Monroe chuckled quietly, Dimp went out of the door, Baby Sis and Woodie laid on each other's shoulders. Even Charles had tears from laughing. I was so embarrassed. I just sat there looking dumb.

Well, that faux pas endeared me to the family. We were married December 29, 1959

They tell this story every chance they get.

My First Car—"Black Beauty"

"Shirley, you can not afford a car. You just started working."
"Oh daddy, it's only $3000. I could make the payments."
Daddy gave up and I bought a 1955 Dodge. It was black with silver wings on the back fenders. The interior was white and aqua leather with a half white and half aqua steering wheel. I was so proud! (I thought I was right cute!) I knew after daddy saw this car, he would change his mind.

On the way home, I stopped for a red light. I just knew I looked good driving this sharp car, when a hearse came around the corner and hit it. Well, I jumped out of the car and started fighting the driver. I was screaming and crying. (I lost all dignity.)

"This is my brand new car! I haven't even got it home and you hit it!" I was still swinging when the police arrived. They called a tow truck and sent my beautiful car back to the showroom garage where I had been 15 minutes ago.

We never know why some things happen. Maybe I forgot Exodus 20:3.

My First Pair of High Heel Shoes

Some things happen in your life that you would like to forget, but can't. We always got new clothes for Easter. This was my year to get grown-up shoes. My plan was to get high heels at last!

"Shirley, you can have a slight heel on your shoes. Don't come back here with any shoes with a real high heel. Do you hear me?"

"Yes, Mama."

I had already seen the shoes I wanted and they did have a higher heel than I knew Mama would like. I took them home to face the music. I knew I could not take them back.

"What did I tell you? Not to get high heels. (Mama had a habit of answering her own questions.) You will have to wear them. I am not giving you any more money. You'll just have to do the best you can. You probably can't even walk in them."

Well, Easter Sunday arrived. I had been invited to attend church with a friend. My father could see I was having trouble with those shoes. He drove me to the church. He said he would come back to pick me up. When I stepped out of the car my heel got caught on the running board. (Cars had something like a step called a running board.) I fell right out on the church pavement. My hat went one way. I went the other. People entering the church had paused to see this sight. Daddy got out of the car, never said a word, picked me up, put me in the car and drove me home. I was crying and very embarrassed. When we got home, my mother did not say, "I told you so!" She hugged me and told me to go put on last year's shoes. She knew I had learned a hard lesson.

My Parents' Night Out

Being the youngest of siblings, my parents were going to being seniors as I was coming into real adulthood. I wanted them to "hang out" with me. I wanted my parents to share some good times with me. To this end, I invited them out for an evening.

First, we went to dinner at the top of the Holiday Inn to the Revolving Restaurant. As we turned, they could see the entire city, the harbor, sailboats and yacht. This was a new experience for them and I was so pleased.

The porter came with the breads and inquired to whether we wanted anything to drink. We put in our orders. My mother ordered a cup of hot tea.

I said, "You always drink tea at home. Order something different."

"Oh, tea is just fine."

There were many types of breads and my mother drank her tea and ate bread. When dinner arrived, my mother was full of tea and bread.

"I've had enough to eat. Please take this back."

The waiter looked at me in shock. I told him to fix it for carryout. My mother could not understand why I would pay for a dinner that she did not want. I told her that I would explain it to her later.

After my father and I finished our dinner, we left to continue our night out. I took them to one of my friend's parents home. There they enjoyed dessert and conversation. Next we went to another friend's home. There, a pinochle game was in progress. All of my friends knew that my parents love to play pinochle, so they invited them to play. A good time was had by all!

About 2a.m., I took them home. They looked at me and said, "Shirley, we really appreciated having this time with you and your friends. We really enjoyed ourselves. But do us a favor. Don't ask us out again. We are just not up to it anymore."

"But, I thought you had a good time."

"We did up until 10'clock"

"Why didn't you tell me?"

"We did not want to disappoint you."

See? That's the kind of parents they were. We always came first with them even if it meant staying out with me four hours after their bedtime.

What a pair!

My South Sea Experience

"Hi Shirley, I found a real good trip for us to take."

"Helena, where, when, and how much?"

"Well, we are going to Los Angeles, New Zealand, Australia and Fiji. We leave October 18th and return November 2nd. It will run around $3000 including a little for spending."

"Yes, a very little. I'll check with Charles and see what he says. I know he will not want to go, but we'll have to discuss the money. I'll call you tonight. I think it will be alright."

Everything went well. Helena and I flew to Los Angeles. We stayed at the Hyatt Hotel at the airport. After dinner we went straight to bed. We knew we faced a long day on Friday.

In the morning after breakfast, we went to Long beach to visit the RMS Queen Mary and the Howard Hughes "Flying Boat, The Spruce Goose." We had a lovely dinner and were returning to the airport for our flight to New Zealand when Helena realized that she had lost her wallet. "Oh, My Lord! I've lost my wallet! I remember taking it out to pay my bill I must have dropped it on the floor instead of putting it in my bag. It has all of my money, passport and everything in it. What am I going to do?"

"Helena, I will talk to the bus driver and see if he can somehow help us out."

I told the driver the problem. "We are too far to go back. Do you know anyone that you can call that might be able to get it if it is still there?" I will radio the restaurant and have them check for it."

He explained the problem. When he called me up front of the bus, he said, "They found it right where you left it. They will hold it for you until it can be picked up."

"May I use your phone, I do have some friends that live here. They might be able to do this and get it to the airport before we have to leave. Hello, Howard? Hi, this is Shirley from Maryland, I am here in Los Angeles heading for New Zealand."

I explained the problem. They left immediately, headed for Long Beach. By this time we were back at the airport. We were to leave at 10:00PM. Helena was so nervous. If my friends did not make it, we could not go without her passport. We were moving toward the gate, when I heard a voice on the speaker calling my name. I knew everything was all right. We hugged, thanked Marilyn and Howard for their help and headed for the plane.

We hadn't gotten out of the US and we already had our first adventure! We crossed the International Date Line on Saturday and lost a day. The flight was so long!

"Helena, If they feed us any more, I am going to burst"

"Same here, but we don't have to eat it. It is so good I can't refuse. The soup, salads, beef, bagels, cheeses, chicken, everything."

"My feet are swelling. We better get up and walk awhile. We can walk down some of the food and eat some more."

"You have the right idea."

After a 15 hour flight, we finally got to New Zealand.

My Two-Day Job

My sister Irene, two of her friends and I wanted a summer job. A person at the office where my father worked said they could get us a job at a private girl's camp in New Hampshire. We would work in the dining room. It sounded good to us, so we accepted the position. We traveled by train to New Hampshire, which was exciting.

When we got to the camp we found it to be very different. The campers arrived in expensive cars with chauffeur. Some brought their own horses. Some had to be picked up from the airport. Every camp I attended meant sleeping in tents. These sleeping quarters looked more like hotel rooms.

In the dining room it was our job to set tables. We had to make sure the bowl and platters that held the food were always full. It was a race to clean up from breakfast and prepare for lunch. The campers could eat leisurely and we could not start cleaning until they were finished.

One morning I was told to report to the owner's cabin. When I arrived, she was propped up on pillows in her bed. The cabin looked like a beautiful hunting lodge.

She said, "You will not work in the dining room anymore. You will be my maid. You will come here every morning and bring my breakfast. Then you will do things I need done."

I couldn't believe what I was hearing. I don't wait on anyone unless they are sick or crippled outside of family and friends. She was neither. This morning it was her wash.

"You must wash my undies today."
"Where is the washing machine?"
"Oh. You have to wash them by hand."

"I don't wash my own by hand."

"You will do as I say or you are fired. I know you can't leave because you have not worked long enough to get any pay."

"Watch me. I'm never sent away from home without a way to get back."

I left and went down to the dining room where my sister was.

"What's the matter?"

"I've been fired for not wanting to be a maid. I'm going home."

"Well if you go, we will go also."

I called my father to tell him that we were coming home.

"What did you do this time?"

When we got home and told what had happened, my father was very upset.

"I sent you there to work in the dining room, not to be some maid. You had a right to leave. You do not have to stand for poor treatment from anyone, rich or poor."

Well, the trip was not a complete waste. We enjoyed the train ride.

The Engagement Ring

Dear Charles,

We will be going to Holland for a weekend. Anne is going to pick out her engagement ring at the Diamond Factory of Amsterdam. Would you mind if I picked out mine at the same time? They are so reasonable here. Please let me know what you think.

Hi Baby,

If you want to get your ring over there, it is fine with me. I am sending you a check. If it is more, let me know. Just one thing; I want you to send it to me and I will give it to you when you get home.

Well, the weekend came and our group went to Amsterdam. We were so excited about going to the diamond factory to pick out our rings. After we checked in to the Bed and Breakfast Inn, we decided to go to Kerkenhoff to see the beautiful tulips.

It is impossible to explain the beauty we beheld as we drove through the gates of Kerkenhoff. There were windmills along the way. There were the Dutch people dressed in the native clothing, even with the wooden shoes.

This was the first time any of us had ever seen black swans. They were so different. There was a field of tulips for each country. The American tulip was a field of white. After a lunch of bread, cheeses and wine, we continued to the Diamond Factory of Amsterdam.

The first thing Anne and I did was to make up our minds what shape of diamond we wanted. We were shown many different shapes. After we made the selection, we followed the entire process of shaping our diamonds. After the diamonds were shaped, we had to choose the ring itself.

When it was all said and done, Anne and I had beautiful diamond rings that we had seen made from start to finish. I will always treasure not just the ring and diamond, but the experience of seeing it made. I know Anne feels the same way.

Yes, Charles was very pleased with the ring and the price!

My Wedding Day

The excitement was high on this special day. Although it was the 27th of December, the weather cooperated by being a warm 72 degrees. My parents' home was adorned with the usual wedding decorations. The caterers had arrived to prepare for the reception. My close friends and I were upstairs dressing for the occasion. This will be a day to remember.

My family and guests started to arrive, but the atmosphere took a plunge from joyful to joyless. The women in the group seemed uncompromising, and the men seemed very upset. After listening to muffled conversation, I discovered that there was a very important football game being played on the same day, at the same time of my wedding. The wives told the husbands that they had to attend the wedding and not go to the football game. At that point, I knew my name was mud!

I had been in Europe teaching for a year and had no idea that the hometown football team was playing the game of the year here at the stadium. Well, the men were not going to miss that game! They began to put lawn furniture, extension cords and televisions in my parents' yard.

At 2 p.m., my wedding started and so did the football game. My future husband's brother, the minister, proceeded with the ceremony. It seemed a little rushed, but I was "in love!" My brother would rush in, take pictures and leave for the yard. I don't have a decent picture. The best man was looking for signals from the guest for the score. My husband heard "you may kiss the bride" which he did, hugged me and said, "I'll be right back". The caterers, the groom, the minister, and all other interested parties were in the yard.

My mother, a very proper lady who knew nothing about football, could not understand what had happened to her well-planned social event. To show her consternation, she stood in the middle of the floor with her hands clutched as if she were about to break out in song said "THIS IS THE BIGGEST MESS I HAVE EVER BEEN INVOLVED IN".

Well, the hometown team won. After the rejoicing, the reception got back to normal. I was finally the center of attraction. As I said at the beginning, "This would be a day to remember," (December 27, 1959) and it was! After 47 years, someone brings it up at the family gatherings.

Once an Actress

A group of frustrated actors and actresses decided to form a theatre group. They started in the basement of a church. This took place in 1953 in Baltimore, Maryland. Today, The Arena Players is the oldest African American Playhouse in the United States. Now, they have a beautiful building and an active following.

I have been an avid supporter of this group since 1953. While I was a student in college, I would promote ticket selling, solicit ads and donations. I was very happy to be a part of all of this. Then one day the director of the play "The Cradle Song" approached me.

"Shirley, I need you to play the part of a nun."

"You have got to be kidding. A nun? My friends would laugh me off the stage. A nun? I am so far from a nun that this would be a complete turnaround. Do you really think I could do it? A nun?"

"I would not have asked you if I didn't think you could do it."

"You asked me because you needed someone, anyone, to play the part!"

"You got me! Please don't say no."

"Well, since you begged me, I will do it."

"I thought you would. Knowing you, you will enjoy being on the stage. We will rehearse tonight at the church around 6 o'clock."

Well, I did fine until the director said, "Shirley, you must go center stage, fall on your knees and cry real tears."

"How am I to cry real tears?'

"When we get finished with these rehearsals, you will cry!"

"When I finish falling on my knees, I'll cry from the pain!"

The play went well. My entire family and a load of friends came to see "the nun."

I did my part, even falling on my knees. And cried real tears. The tears got going and I could not stop them. At curtain call, I had tears rolling down my cheeks. The director said in my ear "ok, Shirley, cut it!" Are they tears of joy or relief?"

"They must be relief. I will never put myself under that pressure again."

My family and friends thought I was great. (They would. They love me.) I went back to selling tickets, soliciting ads and donations. In 1982, I was presented The Arena Players Civic Award.

Now in 2006, I am still a member. I only watch the plays and applaud wildly.

Remembering High School

Entering high school in 1948 was a fearful experience. Everything was so different from Junior. High. The older students seemed hostile. So many students in the halls. Everyone knew where he or she was going except me.

How will I ever fit in here? I decided to join every club that would accept me. When the time came to sign up, I signed for the band, choir, orchestra and drama. I was accepted in all. When the band / orchestra instructor found out that I could not read music, but had a good ear, he was very pleased. "Shirley, I can use you in the marching band to play the glockenspiel. In the orchestra, you will be perfect for the tympani because you will be able to tune them just by listening and using the pedals."

"I have never played either of these instruments, but I am a quick learner." I did learn quickly and had a ball!

In the choir, I could not be heard over so many good voices, so I did not stay there too long. The drama club was called "The Mask and Wig." After a few meetings, we put on the play "You Can't Take It With You." I was given the part of a drunken guest. I would have my sisters help me with my lines. When my mother heard what part I had, she was very upset. "You know we do not drink in our home. What will people think? I do not approve of you doing that part."

"Oh, Mama, she will be good in that part. You know how crazy she can act."

"That's exactly why I don't want her staggering all over the stage with a liquor bottle in her hand. Daddy will certainly agree with me. Ask him when he comes home from work."

"Daddy, I am in a play at school and Mama said I should give the part up. I play a drunk. Daddy, I'm good in the part. Please say that I can do it."

"Well, as long as you are not really drunk, I think you can do it."

"Tom, (that was what Mama called Daddy) you will let that child do anything she wants to. I will not go to the play and watch my child on stage with all of those people looking at her being a drunk."

The night of the play, Mama did not come, but all of the rest of the family was there. The play was a success. I think, looking back, Mama regretted not coming. That was the first and last time she did not support me.

Skipping School

In high school, we think we are grown. We think we are smarter than any adult. Every once in awhile, we decide to try this theory out.

The Royal Theatre was Baltimore's Stage Show Theater. Every Friday at noon, there was a Bargain Hour for 25 cents. One could see two feature movies and the stage show. We could see performers like Nat "King" Cole, Sammy Davis Jr., Sam Cook, The Ravens, and the Orioles. The Temptations, Moms Mably, Ella Fitzgerald, Red Fox, Sarah Vaughn, Billie Holiday, Earl Hines, Cab Callaway and so many more.

Since we were "smart" seniors, we decided to cut class and go to the Bargain Hour. We did not know that other classes had the same idea.

"Let's meet at the door off of the gym. No one is ever back there. Are you going, Shirley?"

"I've never cut school. It will be just my luck to get caught. I don't think I'm going."

"Oh, don't be such a drag. We are all going. They won't even know we are gone. This is our lunch and study period."

Well, I joined the group. We went out of the back door and ran down Pennsylvania Avenue out of sight of the school. Then we casually walked to the theater in time for the first feature, "Imitation of Life." The second feature was a cowboy movie.

From the stage they announced, "Presenting the Orioles." We screamed and applauded wildly. When the lights came up, there was the Vice Principal of our school standing on the stage.

You have never seen any place empty so quickly. I was terrified. "What will my parents say?" We all ran up Pennsylvania Avenue!

What a sight! There must have been a hundred or more students running back to school, with the Vice Principal, the two janitors, counselors and any other adults chasing them.

The first ones to arrive at the school found that all of the doors had been locked. I knew my life was coming to an end. We followed the crowd to one side of the school that had rooms on the first floor that had windows almost down to the ground. I will never know how I got through the window. Once again, I must have had a guardian angel.

This was such a traumatic experience for me. That was the first and last time I tried that trick.

Switzerland

Continuing our Christmas vacation, we headed to Zurich, Switzerland. What a beautiful city. One look and one could tell that this was a ski country. The mountains surrounded the city. There were many ski lifts going up and down the mountains non-stop.

"Now, people, we have got to do better here than we did in Italy. Look at those mountains. They are bigger and taller than any we have seen."

"Ok Shirley. Let's find the hotel and see if there is room for us. Let's stay here two days. That will give us plenty of time to get back to Germany."

We found rooms. Right outside the window you could see the skiers going up and down the mountains. We put on our outfits (we had the nerve to have ski outfits) and made it out to get ready for the big run down the mountain. The workers at the lifts had good sense. They put us in the beginners lift and told us we could not go any higher since we did not know how to ski. How did they know? We looked scared.

The beginners' slopes were a little much, but we managed to have a good time. When we had enough, we decided to go shopping, after which we decided to take a ride to the top of a mountain in a cable car. It took the cable car about 15 minutes to reach the top. On the way up we were told that there was a trail that one could follow back to the lodge. Some of the people said they were going back by the trail. We might as well do the same. We did not realize what we had chosen to do. I was carrying a music box and the others had bags that they had purchased.

After three hours we finally got back to the hotel, worn out. We ate dinner and went straight to bed. In the morning, none of us could get out of the bed.

"Elaine, can you move?

"No. I feel like I am paralyzed. What has happened to us?"

"I'll call down to the desk and ask for a doctor."

After we told the doctor that we had walked down the mountain, he laughed.

"No wonder you can't move. You used muscles you didn't know you had. A few days in bed and you will be your old self again."

Emily, who was very hyper, told the doctor, "We can't stay here, we are due back to school in Germany in a few days!"

"Well, you will have to do the best you can, because there is nothing I can do. Some of your muscles have been strained and will take time to heal."

He felt so sorry for us that he said "No Charge."

We finally got to the train, walking like zombies. In a few days we all were better and ready to get back to work.

The Bomb Scare

A group of friends boarded the plane at BWI heading for Florida for a 19-day cruise. In the news there was a lot of talk about bomb scares in buildings, on buses and on planes. We took that news with a grain of salt. Nothing like that could happen on our trip.

"Nothing ever happens in Baltimore. We're only flying to Florida."

"Shirley, you don't believe anything you hear. I wish I was that sure."

"Oh, don't worry. Come on. It's time to board."

We were enjoying the flight when the announcement came that we were going to land in North Carolina because of an emergency.

"Please fasten your seatbelts and return your tray tables to the upright position"

I don't know why, but everyone in the group was looking at me!

After landing, we were removed from the plane in minutes. We were ushered into a transfer bus. There, we got the reason for the emergency.

"There has been a report of a bomb on the plane. We have landed in a field away from the terminal. You will be seated in a private room until you name is called. Your luggage will be opened in the field. You must come out, remove all belongings and the dogs will sniff for the bomb. After which, you must repack your bags. They will be placed back on the plane. You may return to the plane or you may wait in the terminal until the plane has been cleared. We have notified the ships of the problem. They will hold up the sailing time. Thank you for your cooperation."

It took hours for this process to be completed. Finally the announcement came for our plane to leave. We boarded again and headed for our vacation.

We found out that on our flight was a bride and groom. The call had come from a requited love of the bride. The rest of the trip went well. The ship waited. I had another adventure to talk about. To me, it was exciting!

The Bravest Man I Had Ever Known

His name was Charles Hilary Griffin, my beloved husband. We were in high school together. We were married for 38 years, 11 months, 23 days. During that time, he developed diabetes, high blood pressure and cancer. He suffered strokes, diabetic comas and lost his right leg to diabetes. He had cancer of the throat and had to have a metal jaw. Charles ate liquefied food for five years. With this trauma going on in his life, he never complained about any thing. He was happy and continues to live his life. He learned to drive with his left foot. He traveled with me, went to his lodge meeting and conventions, was an usher at church, entertained at home at dinners and picnics and did any thing he wanted to do.

When the cancer spread to his lungs, the doctor told him he had three months to live. He wanted to know if they could operate. The doctor told him yes, but that would only extend his life three more months. He chose the operation.

The nicest, sweetest, most wonderful thing Charles ever said to me was that he went through all of the operations and pain because he did not want to leave me. He wanted to stay with me as long as he could and all he had gone through was worth it.

It has been nine years since he left me. It still hurts.

The Bus Trip from Hell

"Shirley, why don't you plan a bus trip to Canada?" was the question asked me as soon as the bus stopped.

"We just got back from Hilton Head. Would you mind if I got a rest?"

"We would like to go next month. That should be enough rest for you."

"Gee, thanks. That is so big of you. You are never satisfied! I'll see what I can do."

Of course the group knew that I would plan the trip. I always did. (They knew that I just love to be in charge!) Calling the bus company, picking the date, collecting the money and planning the itinerary. All of that was right down my alley.

Well, June 21st arrived. There were 42 people traveling this time. The luggage that these people brought for a week's trip was unbelievable! Poor Chuck, our bus driver, loaded not only the luggage, but all of my paraphernalia; Bingo game, Karaoke Machine, a guitar, CDs, breakfast food, water, sodas, snacks, plastic items and a few other things that I would need to run a successful trip.

We left right on time, heading for Boston. The bus broke down right outside of Boston.

Another company sent a bus to bring us into the city. Poor Chuck had to transfer all of that "stuff" to the new bus. We were only supposed to be in Boston for a few hours. We stayed two days waiting for our bus to be repaired. The sad news came that our bus could not be repaired and we would have to continue our trip in the borrowed bus.

WAS IT A DREAM

Everything was going well. I decided to have a cocktail party! As I was serving the sparkling cider, one of my heavier ladies decided to use the rest room. As she was returning to her seat, the bus swerved trying to miss a car. This made the lady lose her balance, came down the aisle full force, heading right for me. I was knocked in the floor, my ear got cut on the seat handle, but I held on to the bottle! "Are you hurt, Shirley?"

"Oh, no, I'm fine." (I was lying through my teeth!)

We finally got to Bar Harbor, Maine. I got everyone settled (still grinning), went in to the manager's office, laid across his desk, crying, and asked him to take me to the hospital.

At the hospital, nine stitches were put in my ear. The doctor gave me Tylenol 3, which as you know will put you to sleep. (How do you run a bus trip asleep?)

The next morning we went to Peggy's Cove. Although I was drugged, I could read the big sign that said, "DO NOT CLIMB ON THE ROCKS". One person had to try anyway, and twisted her ankle. After a day there, we checked into our hotel. I was so tired. As I was on the elevator going to my room, some of my people were going to play cards in their rooms. I was so glad that everyone was in the hotel, happy and safe.

I had just gotten in bed when the phone rang. "Is this Shirley Griffin?"

"Yes".

"This is the hospital calling to let you know one of the ladies on your trip fell in the mall and broke her hip. Please come to identify her and contact her family. I could have cried! I had just taken a pill.

When I arrived at the hospital, I saw the one with the broken hip. She was not very friendly. As I left her room, in the hall was the one who hurt her ankle, sitting with a cast up to her knee. It was broken. I could not believe this! I just knew all of my people were in their rooms at the hotel.

After checking everything out, I headed back to the hotel. It was almost morning. I finally got in my bed, and the phone rang. I answered.

This voice said, "Shirley, I can't wake Thelma up. Please come to my room. I think she is dead."

"What do you mean dead?"

I went to the room and she was dead. (This was the straw that broke the camel's back). I could not believe that so many things could go wrong on a trip. I vowed and declared that this was the last bus trip for me.

Now, remember, I started out with 42 people. So far, I have two in the hospital, one dead, two staying with the body and two that decided to fly home. The group is getting smaller by the day. The atmosphere on that bus was depressing. We had never experienced anything like this before.

Well, we headed home. We crossed back to the mainland on the Blue Nose Ferry. The water was very rough and the rain was coming down very hard. The ferry docked, the bus came off and we headed for our overnight motel.

Chuck had a time driving with the rain beating so hard against the windshield. He asked me to come up to the front of the bus and keep him company. The bus sounded strange, although it was still moving. Chuck said, "I will tell you something if you promise not to get upset."

I assured him that after what had already happened, nothing would upset me. He quietly said, "The bus gears are locked and will not change."

What else could happen? We got to the overnight motel. Someone had called home and reported the death, but did not know the name of the person. When I checked in at the front desk, 28 telephone calls from Baltimore were waiting for me. "Who died"?

Chuck spent most of the night getting the bus repaired. I can only imagine what he was thinking!

We finally arrived home. As the ladies were getting off of the bus, two teenagers snatched a purse. As they were running away, two other teenagers saw this and snatched it back (I think that HE is trying to tell me something, like don't run anymore trips!)

You would think that I had learned my lesson. Oh no! In the fall, we went north to see the changing of the leaves. How soon we forget.

The Day Elvis Arrived at Campo Pond

First, I must tell you that Campo Pond is a training area for soldiers stationed in Hanau, Germany. It was right in the middle of the grounds where the school for the military children was located. I taught the fourth grade there.

As soon as I arrived at the school this particular morning, I was met with pupils yelling "Elvis is coming to Campo Pond this afternoon."

"Who told you that?"

"My father is in his squad and he told me?"

That was the talk all over the school. The high school students let it be known that they were not coming back to school after lunch. (Everyone had an hour and a half for lunch because the students went home for lunch.)

When it was time for school to start after lunch, the school was empty of pupils. Since there was no one to teach, all of the teachers, principal and other staff went to see Elvis also. We took pictures and had a day with Elvis.

Thought to Be Algerian

One of my friends fell in love with one of the officers in Hanau. I was invited to the wedding, which was to be held in Zurich, Switzerland. It seems that if an American got married in Germany, they would have to pay some type of tax. To alleviate this, Switzerland was the chosen place for weddings.

The trip going was great. The wedding was wonderful. Returning home was a scary experience. I was traveling alone on a bus. Everything went well until we got to the French Border. When the officers came aboard the bus to check our passports, they told me to get off the bus. I did not speak French and I really did not know what they wanted.

I was taken into the office and questioned.

"What is your name?"

"Shirley Johnson."

"Why are you trying to enter France?"

"I am going back to Germany. My passport explains my business in Germany."

"Your passport says you are American. You are Algerian. Black people in America are too poor to travel unless they are in the service."

By this time I was really scared. I tried to understand what they were saying in French to no avail.

A German doctor came into the office. "This lady is an American citizen. She is not Algerian. The American Embassy will not understand your treatment of a citizen like this."

"Get back on the bus and don't come this way again."

"You have no right to tell her she can not travel this way again. You will be reported to your embassy. I am (he gave some name that caused some concern among the group.)"

"Please accept our apology."

I was escorted back to the bus. By this time I was upset and just wanted to get back to Germany. No more weddings for me!

The Egypt Adventure

The entire trip was an adventure. First, our luggage was lost on our way to the cruise ship in Greece. We were to cruise from Greece to India, with ports in between. Every time we left a port, the message would come saying that our luggage had just arrived at that port. This went on for 5 days. We finally got the luggage.

The ship docked at a port that was an 8-hour drive from Egypt. Those passengers that were to go to see the Pyramids had to go by bus and meet the ship in the next port.

"Come on Doris, the buses are loading up. Hurry and say goodbye to Austin. I'll find Charles. They are going to be sorry that they are not going with us. Neither one of them wanted the bus ride, but I want to see the Pyramids."

We boarded the buses and waved goodbye to the people left on the ship. There were 8 buses following each other. As we were riding along, out of the window you could see towers with soldiers along the road. When we questioned our guide, he explained that some tourist buses had been attacked the week before. The soldiers were for our protection. Of course this was very upsetting to the group.

"Why were we not told about this before we left the ship?"

"Because the tour agency knew that most of you would change your mind. They have done everything to ensure your safety. Please do not let this ruin your trip to Egypt. You are being well protected."

The trip went well. Of course, we were not relaxed, but we arrived at Cairo safely. After checking into the hotel, we had a wonderful dinner and off to see the Light Show at the Pyramids.

"Shirley, I am about to freeze out here in this desert. Who would have thought it would be this cold here?"

"I'm glad we could rent blankets or we would freeze to death. I'm not too happy about using this blanket, but it is better than nothing."

The Light Show was beautiful. We returned to our hotel for a midnight snack. By this time we were ready for bed. Our rooms were very cold. We called down to the desk to see if we could get some heat. That is when we found out that the hotels do not have heat It was a miserable night.

The next morning after a breakfast of breads, cheeses, fruit, coffee, tea and pastries, we headed back to the pyramids to see what they looked like in the daytime. We were not disappointed. They were magnificent, unbelievable and huge. We could not enter any of them because security was tight. We were told not the ride the camels and to stay close to the group.

When we were ready to go, one passenger was missing. The guides searched high and low, to no avail. They decided to take another look because we could not leave without her. They finally found her on a camel. The driver would not lower the camel for her to get off unless she gave him $100. She was crying and very scared. The tour guides reprimanded the driver and had him arrested.

"We told you not to ride the camels. We cannot be responsible when you do not follow our directions. What you did was very dangerous."

"I asked the driver if I could get a picture sitting on the camel. I had no idea that he would take me away from the group. I am so sorry."

When it was time to return to the ship, we boarded the buses and headed back. Again, we saw the towers and soldiers along the road. There were no cars, trucks or buses on that road. The buses zigzaged and changed positions until we arrived at the ship. We again asked the guide why this was happening.

"We got a report that it could be trouble going back. The drivers were instructed to change bus positions back to the ship."

When we found Charles and Austin, they were very worried about us.

"Austin and I wished you both had not gone. Following the last bus was a convoy of Egyptian soldiers. That is when we found out about the trouble with the other tour buses.

We are so glad things went ok, but we should have been told about the trouble. Neither one of you would have gone."

"It was worth the trip to see what you only read about. I'm glad we went."

"You would be, Shirley. You like a lot of excitement. She was in her world. Everyone else was scared. She was calling it an adventure."

"It was! Now, I have something to talk about. The trip was great!"

Venezuela

Visiting Venezuela was a "real trip". There are two experiences that I will never forget. One was a trip to the Venezuela Race Track. I am not a lover of racetracks although I am a Marylander.

Our cab driver in Venezuela said, "I want you to see our horse racing here. You need to see how we do."

"Will we have time to get to see the city, go shopping and get back to the ship on time?"

"Yes, this won't take long. It is a quick race. We will only stay for one run."

"Ok Charles. We are in your hands."

First of all, there is no admission charge. One can enter any kind of horse one chooses. There were swayback horses, thin horses, overweight horses, and any kind of horse you may imagine.

"Are they the horses that are in the race? They look sick."

"Some are, but they will run."

The horses are lined up at the starting point. There is no starting gate. The gun is sounded. The horses, most of them, start running. Some just stand and their riders are beating on them to run. Some that start to run might turn around and try to go the other way.

After the race got underway, an ambulance followed the horses and a horse wagon followed the entire group. I wondered why this was happening. Well, I soon found out.

Some of the horses fell on the track and threw their riders to the ground. The horse wagon would pick up the horses and the ambulance picked up the riders. The race is run until the last horse is standing. There is no pay. It is just that your horse was the best.

"This is the craziest thing I have ever seen."

When we got through laughing, we got back in the cab to continue our day.

The next experience was a little frightening. The ship docked on one side of this huge mountain. To get to the city of Caracas, one either had to drive around the mountain or go over the mountain in a cable car. Of course, we chose the cable.

Going over was great. We got to Caracas and had a wonderful time shopping. When it was time to go back to the ship, we got on the cable car. At the highest point in the air, the cable car stopped. We were swinging in mid air.

The natives did not seem to mind. They could see that we were getting upset.

"Don't worry. This happens all of the time. The electricity went out. It will come back soon."

"How soon? We are on the ship you see down there."

From where we were, one could see the ship and passengers boarding.

"Well, it could be a minute or a couple of hours."

In about fifteen minutes the cable car started down the mountain. We had about ten minutes before the gangway was removed. Once again, my angels were with me.

The Penguin Parade

While traveling in Australia, I had the opportunity to see the real "Penguin Parade." After an interesting day in Melbourne, we traveled to the fishing town of San Remo and crossed the bridge to Phillip Island, Victoria. At dusk we could see far off in the distance hundreds of penguins swimming toward us. All of the visitors were standing above the beach on a raised stand the length of the Summerland Beach.

"Look at all those penguins coming toward us. I have never seen so many at one time."

"How many do you think are out there? It looks like a thousand."

"I did not know that they could swim like that."

The penguins came ashore to visit their burrows in the sand dunes on the beach. As it got dark, the procession was lit and children could sit within a few feet of the parade.

"Watch these over here. They are fighting. Look, look, they are really going at it. I'll ask the guide what's happening."

"There is a fight if a penguin found another in their burrow or if a penguin decided he liked another female penguin. They will fight until one or the other gives up."

"How do you keep up with what is going on with them?"

"The penguins followed a monthly schedule for different activities such as burrow attendance (which was a type of protecting the home), nest building, egg laying, chick raising and molting."

"I see these little penguins have feathers. How do they swim?"

"Penguins are flightless birds that have wings and feathers, but the wings evolve into Flippers."

"What do they eat? Do you have to feed them or do they gather their own food?"

"They have a diet of small fish. The babies grow in eight weeks and are put on their own to swim in the sea, knowing by instinct how to swim and catch food. Please ask me any other questions you might have. It has been a pleasure to have you visit us tonight. Please come again."

This was one of the most interesting tours that I experienced in Australia.

The Retreat at Happy Ours

My Bible Study group had overnight religious retreats twice a year at the Retreat Center of Port Deposit. I enjoyed attending these sessions very much. My husband was recuperating from an operation. I would not be able to attend the retreat that was scheduled for February.

"Shirley, this is Rev. I am going to bring the retreat to your home instead of going to Port Deposit."

"Rev, I can't have that many people here overnight. I only have one bedroom. Where am I going to put 20 people?"

"You have a large basement. I am going to send some cots down in a few days. Ask Austin, Doris and Pauline if they would sleep a few people. The idea came to me from On High. I feel that you and Charles need this blessing. Both of you have been going through a lot. It will be good to have our group in prayer in your home. You might as well get use to the idea because it is going to happen. I'll talk to you soon."

"Ok, Rev if you say so. I hope it works."

Well, in a few days, the cots arrived and were set up in the basement. That Friday evening, people started to arrive. By dark, there were 35 people here for the retreat.

"Come on Lil. Let's select our cots before they are all taken. I don't want to stay anywhere else."

"Come on, Audrey. Tell Ellen we are going downstairs."

I was amazed how everyone just fell right into this unusual situation. Ed, Johnnie, Lil, Barbara and Rev were the cooks for the weekend.

After a dinner of hot dogs, beans, salad, drinks and dessert, we had our first gathering. We were on the floor, furniture, folding chairs, etc.

Rev opened with prayer. What a wonderful feeling to have all of your friends in prayer for YOU!

After the gathering, we had free time. Some played cards, some went for a walk, and some went to bed, while others sang songs around the organ.

The sleeping arrangements could not have gone any smoother. The men slept in sleeping bags in the bedroom with Charles. Rev slept on the couch in the family room. The ladies were downstairs or in other homes. In the morning, I woke my guests up with organ music. I started to worry about how the bathrooms were going to work out with 27 people and 2 bathrooms. There was not one problem. It all worked like magic. The cooks served a breakfast of bacon, eggs, biscuits, fried apples, grits, tea and coffee. Lunch was fruit, sandwiches, and drinks.

The other sessions went well. The most touching activity was when the men went to the basement, removed the cots, set up my long folding tables and folding chairs. Some of the ladies put on white tablecloths. Rev prepared the table for communion with a loaf of round homemade bread and wine. We shared communion as our closing of the retreat.

When it was time to depart, we all left feeling fresh and clean in spirit.

"Where two or three gather……" Yes, He was there.

The School of Horrors

My mother was raised around Episcopal Nuns. She was always talking about the wonderful times she had spent with them.

"I want the three of you (Mary, Irene, Shirley) to have that experience. So Daddy and I are going to send you to an Episcopal School in Pennsylvania for two weeks. This will be a nice way for you to do something different this summer."

We looked forward to going until we saw the school. It was an old gray cement building with a wall around it. It looked like a prison. The Nuns greeted us, and checked us in. We bid our parents goodbye (we should have gone with them) and we were shown to our rooms. We were put into different areas according to age. That meant we were separated. This was hard on me because I was only 6 and I was used to being around my sisters.

We had to get up at 6a.m., go to mass at 7a.m. and eat breakfast at 8a.m. This particular morning, we had melted three-flavor ice cream over our oatmeal. Work the rest of the morning. We had to work in the kitchen or garden or clean toilets, wash floors, do laundry or any other chore that the Nuns thought of.

I was under punishment most of the time. When I went to mass, I always got sick from the incense. I was punished. The toilets had to be flushed with buckets of water. The buckets were too heavy for me to carry, so I would drag it to the toilet. By the time I got to the toilet, the water I had left was not enough in which to flush, so I had to keep going back until I put in enough to flush. Of course the water was on the floor. The Nuns would not let me have any help. I got punished. The punishment was to be sent to your room during "free" time. (Ha)

When I was punished, I would go to my room and sing my favorite song, "Glow Worm" as loud as I could. Of course I was punished for that.

If you wrote a letter to your parents, it was read before you could mail it. My older sister was determined to get a letter out. So, one day she was put on the shopping detail. She wrote a letter and hid it on her person. When she got outside, she asked someone to please mail it for her. It had no stamp on it, so she did not know if the person would do it. We just prayed that they would.

Our prayers were answered. One day we were called to the Nun's office and there sat our father. The Nun vowed and declared that she did not know why we wanted to go home before the two weeks were up.

When we got home and shared our experience with our parents, my mother cried. She was so hurt that she had entrusted us to people that she thought she could trust with her children.

Things were so different back there in my parents' time. Parents were more trusting of people. It was a simpler time. Things were slowly changing to where we are today. Check out everyone and everything.

The Table Turns

If your parents live to an old age, it is a blessing. It becomes the children's responsibility to care for them. It was a pleasure to care for our parents. They were so willing to make things easy for us. Whatever was suggested they would go along. When we felt it was time for them to give up their home, they only asked, "when and where do you want us to live?"

They moved into an apartment and really enjoyed the change. A few years after that we told our father it was time for him to stop driving. No problem. We saw to it that they got where they wanted to go.

With six siblings cooperating, no one was overwhelmed. Daddy became ill with cancer. All of us were working except my two older sisters. They would be with our parents while we worked. After we got off, we would take over. A schedule was worked out so that our parents would not be alone. At night someone was with them.

My father "crossed over." My mother was heartbroken. They had been married 60+ years. We moved Mama to another apartment in another building. She did not mind the move. Soon, Mama became ill. We were there to take care of her. One day she had to go to the hospital. We were all there when the doctor came out of the room laughing. He came over to us and said "In all of my professional career, I had never been asked to encourage children to put a mother in a nursing home. Your mother said that all of you were doing the best you could. You were excellent in your jobs, but you did not know anything about nursing."

We were hurt. We did not want to put our mother in a nursing home.

The doctor said, "With your mother being heavy, when you have to lift her, not knowingly, you hurt her. In a nursing home they would move her in a hoist."

We took her home and asked her if that was really what she wanted. It was agreed that we would find the best one for her. I had heard about a nursing home that was very nice. I visited and was impressed. I asked for an application. The lady in charge of admittance said, "It is no sense for you to take an application, there is a two-year waiting list."

"I'll take one anyway. Something might open up."

She was not too pleased, but she gave it to me. I don't know why, but I felt I had to get that application back to her as soon as possible. I took it back the next day.

About four days later, we were with Mama and the phone rang. It was for me.

"Hello, yes, this is she."

"This is the nursing home. We would like for you to bring your mother here today. Please bring her in an ambulance. We will be waiting for her."

We could not believe it. What happened to the two-year wait? We got to the nursing home with Mama in tow. She was taken to a private room with bath. We were so pleased that she was pleased. Of course, our schedule transferred to the nursing home and she was never alone except at night.

Charles and I were coming up to our 25th wedding anniversary. We had planned a 10 days cruise. Our anniversary was December 27th.

We told Mama that we did not have to go. "We can stay home and celebrate right here. We would not lose any money."

"No, I want you to go. You will only have one 25th Anniversary and I want you to go and not worry about me I'll be here when you get back."

We sailed on December 23rd at 6p.m. Mama "crossed over" Christmas Eve at 3:30a.m. When we called home, I was told that everything was fine. My sister asked to speak to Charles. She said she wanted to know how he liked the ship. She actually told him that Mama was gone. It was up to him whether he would tell me. That sweet man carried that burden until we were heading home. He did not want to ruin things for me.

The memorial service was held after we returned home. It took me a while to forgive myself for not being here. A minister friend asked me, "When did God say He needed your help. If He had wanted you here, you would have been here."

That helped, but I still think about it.

What a New Year Eve!

It was 1962. We were looking forward to a great 1963. Charles had decided to not hang out early as was his habit every New Year's Eve Day. He would come home in time to dress and we would head out for the midnight gala.

"How come you are not hanging with your boys today? If you stay home, they will be calling all day."

"No they won't. We decided to rest because tonight will be enough. We are saving it all for tonight."

Well, things went well. I continued to get the house in order for the New Year. My mother always said, "The way your home looks on New Year's Day will be the way it looks all year. All of your clothes should be cleaned and ironed."

Of course I believe Mama year after year although my home did not stay clean all year and I always had clothes to wash and iron. But Mama said and I believed it. Things went well all day. We both had time to rest before it was time to go out for the evening. I fed Coco, our poodle; we got dressed and went across the road to the party.

The party was in full swing when someone looked over to my house and yelled" FIRE, FIRE!"

"Oh, My Lord! Coco is in there. Get my dog, please someone get my dog!"

One of the guests said, "Her house is on fire and she is worrying about a dog."

"You shut up! Charles, Charles! Coco is going to die. Tell the firemen to get Coco!"

The men at the party all ran to help. They moved the cars out of the carport and helped the firemen pump water from the fire truck

(We had well water). They kept the people back from the live wires that had fallen. One of the guests who had been drinking got by the men and yelled, "I'll save her. I'll save the child!" (He thought Coco was a child.) As he ran over the lawn, he stepped on one of the live wires. He went straight up in the air screaming. The next time we saw him, he was back at the party house sitting in a chair, sober. Coco was found in his bed dead. I cried so hard. I think Charles wanted to cry also, but you know how men are. (He cried later.)

The fire was finally put out. The fire chief said the one of the electric candles had a break in the cord and ignited the couch that was near it.

"Take anything out tonight that you will need. We are going to board up the place. Be sure to call your insurance person tonight. They will have someone here tomorrow morning."

Through my tears I said, "I need to take my chitterlings, cake, potato salad, greens and sweet potatoes over to Austin's house. Coco and our clothes are gone. There is nothing to take but food."

Charles got what I wanted and we went over to Austin and Doris' home. The next morning the insurance men came and told us we had nothing to worry about. They sent a large trailer and put it beside our home. I really loved the trailer. It had a living room, two bedrooms, a living room and a small dining nook.

That afternoon, 15 of my friends with whom I teach came down to cheer me. When I saw them, I broke down in tears. Margaret said, "Shirley, if you are going to cry, please put on your wig! You're scaring us."

Of course that made everyone laugh, which was good. We ate and realized that although the fire was bad, things could have been worse. Of all that was lost, Coco, my poodle, was all that I missed.

Valentine for a Lifetime

February 14, 1960 was the first Valentine's Day Charles and I shared as husband and wife. Charles gave me a lovely Valentine card. I was so pleased with it and it was so beautiful that I told him never to buy another one. I would keep this one forever. It is a large card with a pink border with an outline of a white heart in the middle. Inside that white heart, poking out like a tiny pillow is a satin heart with two roses.

The card read:
> A valentine for my Wonderful Wife
> Tell you, Dear, most lovingly
> You mean the world and all to me.
> With Love, Chas

With the card I received a necklace with a wooden heart that he had made. My name is carved on one side. On the other side are the words " My Heart Belongs To You." On a smaller heart are our initials.

I displayed my card and necklace every year even after Charles crossed over in 1997. The card is still in great shape. It will be 46 years old this Valentine's Day. At the end of the month I will place my treasures in their container until next year. It really has been a Valentine for a lifetime.

Trip to West Berlin

This was in 1958. I went to teach for the US Government. I lived and worked in Hanau, Germany. My housemates and I traveled as much as we could on weekends and during holidays.

This trip was to East Berlin, before the wall. Borders separated the east from the west. We decided to drive to West Berlin. We felt safe doing this because every fifteen miles, there were American soldiers guarding our borders. When we reached West Berlin, we decided to walk around the city to see the sights. When evening came, we saw an Opera House on the other side of the street. We decided to go to the opera.

We wanted to purchase the tickets for the balcony. We were not dressed for the evening and we thought we could fit in the upper area.

Jerri said, "I would like six balcony tickets, please."

"Thank you."

We went in and instead of being ushered to the balcony; we were ushered to the first floor. The first three rows of people were moved. They were dressed in evening clothes. We were ordered to SIT!! We were seated in the middle of the first row with soldiers on each side. The next two rows were emptied of people.

After the opera, Boris Guddenoff, we were led to the door with soldiers in the front and back. No one else in the theatre moved. When we got to the door, the doorman said, "Go to the other side of the street, NOW!" On the other side of the street was a crowd of people yelling, "Come over here, come over here." With all of that encouragement, we decided to cross the street. We didn't know that when we crossed the street to the Opera House we were in East Berlin. We did not know that a street separated the east from the west. When we got over to the other side of the street, the people applauded. Some of them saw us go in to the Opera House and watched for us the entire time.

There is a song that says "All night, all day, angels are watching over me." I'm a believer!

Someone once wrote:

Life is not a journey to the grave
with the intention of arriving safely
in a pretty well preserved body,
but rather to skid in broadside,
thoroughly used up,
totally worn out, and proclaiming,
"Wow, what a ride!!!"

Also available from PublishAmerica
SLEEP TIGHT
by Barbara Wagner

Attractive Caryl Stewart, a western artist, has inherited a fortune and fallen in love with David Eagle, the confident and sensual man of her dreams. When her flamboyant, oil-rich great-aunt, Savannah Buckman, dies, the young redhead travels from Scottsdale, Arizona, to manage her great-aunt's estate in upscale Winter Park near Oklahoma City. After a disturbing secret from Savannah's past is revealed and a manipulative friend, almost Caryl's exact twin, becomes the third victim, Caryl knows she is the target of a cunning killer, an unknown murderer who is slowly going insane. Tormented by Oklahoma wind and trapped in the eerie atmosphere of a mysterious mansion, she struggles to escape from a maze of terror, revenge and murder. When her Native American lover is accused, Caryl makes a startling discovery and a cruel psychopath prepares to combine her death with his pleasure.

Paperback, 289 pages
6" x 9"
ISBN 1-60610-096-3

About the author:

Both a writer and an artist, Barbara Wagner lives with her husband in a suburb of Kansas City close to their grown children. She grew up in Oklahoma, has a degree in fine art from the University of Oklahoma, and studied creative writing at Butler University in Indianapolis. An award-winning artist, her work was marketed in Scottsdale, Arizona, for many years. Though *Sleep Tight* is entirely a work of fiction, the artistic life of the novel's protagonist, Caryl Stewart, is drawn from Barbara's own experience and adds a strong framework to the suspenseful story.

Available to all bookstores nationwide.
www.publishamerica.com

Also available from PublishAmerica

EMILLEE KART AND THE SEVEN SAVING SIGNS
THE TALE OF BEASLEY'S BONNET

by Vanessa Wheeler

From the minute she met her eccentric missionary aunt, Emillee Kart's life would never be the same. During their first lunch at the Butterfly Café, Emillee is inducted into a secret club known as the Monarch's Army; minutes later she is running for her life. Not only is Emillee launched into an age-old battle between the Skywalkers and the Hexiums, she may very well be the key to saving the Earthtreadors. Twelve years ago, on the day Emillee was born, a prophecy spread throughout the land of a child that would turn the tide of the battle. Five children were born on that day; two have disappeared. The Hexiums will stop at nothing to eliminate any threat to their victory. Emillee needs to learn who she is in order to help uncover the clues that will bring the Skywalkers closer to their goal.

Paperback, 202 pages
5.5" x 8.5"
ISBN 1-4241-8597-1

About the author:

Love of fantasy combined with spiritual conviction guided this mother of three to spin this faith-based tale. Joanne Strobel-Cort, born in Bethlehem, Pennsylvania, now lives in Summit, New Jersey, with her husband and three children. She works on Wall Street and is a committed Sunday school teacher who relies on faith to meet the challenges of each day.

Available to all bookstores nationwide.
www.publishamerica.com

Also available from PublishAmerica

DOVIE
A TRIBUTE WRITTEN BY HER SON

by Ken Eichler

Paperback, 142 pages
5.5" x 8.5"
ISBN 1-60672-171-2

My first recollections of my life was when I had just turned three. I was in an orphanage and my mama was crying. I didn't know why. She was just crying and I wanted her to feel better. As I grew a little older in the orphanage, I realized what it was all about. I had become three and the rules were that a child could no longer stay in the room with their mother after that. They had to be transferred to a dormitory with other children of about the same age and sex. I believe that was when my mama firmly made up her mind to leave the orphanage to seek a new husband and a new home where we could all live together again. It didn't exactly work out that way and it was a crushing blow to Mama. But that had become the norm for my mama and grandparents. They all had lived their lives from birth in dirty, dark and dangerous mining camps, going through one mine explosion that killed 30 of their friends and acquaintances. And shortly thereafter, losing several loved ones to a national and worldwide devastating disease. And traumatic deaths followed my mama and grandma throughout their lives, even my daddy, who died at the age of 40 of bee stings that left my mama with six small children, including me at the age of three weeks. But we had a Savior that led us to the greatest fraternal organizations in the world, and still the greatest ones in existence today—The Masonic Fraternity and The Order of the Eastern Star. A large part of my story deals with our lives and experiences in the Home they built for us, as well as the lives and experiences of hundreds more who came there to live with us. My mama and my grandma spent almost a lifetime in abject poverty and grief when, except for fate, they would have been among the wealthy and aristocratic families in Birmingham and Jefferson County. I have often wondered: what, exactly, went wrong?

Available to all bookstores nationwide.
www.publishamerica.com

Also available from PublishAmerica

CAUGHT MIDSTREAM
by Uta Christensen

In *Caught Midstream*, Janos, a successful executive, reveals the untold experiences of his youth quite unexpectedly to Sparrow—a young woman he is attracted to. She is allowed to relive his epic journey and becomes drawn into an unnerving yet moving tapestry of travails and extraordinary events that take place in prisoner-of-war camps deep within Russia. Taken by force at age sixteen from the protective circle of his family in Germany, Janos is tossed into the cataclysmic, last-gasp efforts of World War II. His journey takes him to a place of darkness, where he lives through a near-death experience and goes through physical and emotional starvation, hard labor, and ostracism; yet it also carries him into unlikely places and relationships where friendship, compassion, healing, mentoring, and love can, amazingly, still flourish. As the story unfolds, Janos's journey accelerates from adolescence into manhood. Almost miraculously, Janos survives while vast numbers of his co-travelers perish.

Paperback, 271 pages
6" x 9"
ISBN 1-4241-0967-1

About the author:

Born in Germany, Uta Christensen spent years in Ireland, New Zealand, and Australia but settled permanently in California. Holding a B.A. in English and German literature, she taught English at a community college and was an administrative analyst at the University of California. Her first book, her father's memoir, was published in Germany.

Available to all bookstores nationwide.
www.publishamerica.com